MURDER IN THE WIND

A Novel By
DAVE VIZARD

Also by Dave Vizard
A Formula for Murder
A Grand Murder

About this novel

This is a work of fiction. Names, characters, places, and incidents are either the product of the author's imagination or used fictitiously. Any resemblance to actual persons, living or dead, business establishments, events, or locales is entirely coincidental.

Credits

Edited by: Christina M. Frey, J.D., Christina@pagetwoediting.com
Cover photo by Bill Diller, bdiller924@hotmail.com
Back photo by Tyler Liepprandt, michiganskymedia@gmail.com
Design and formatting: Duane Wurst, duane0w@gmail.com
ISBN 978-0-692-97367-7
Printed in the United State of America

Acknowledgements:

MURDER IN THE WIND is largely a Huron County production. This story could not have been created without the help of many hands. In addition to the very talented and skilled artists noted earlier in the book's credits, I relied on the experience, knowledge and expertise of many others throughout the area. My thanks to Janis Stein, Richard Bass, Dennis Collins, Michele LaPorte, Jon Barrett, Rich Jeric, Capt. Tom Carriveau, and Ben Willenberg.

Dedication

For Mickey and Mack. A dad could not be prouder of his sons than I am of these two fine young men.

Chapter 1

Tom Huffmann stuffed the cement-filled chunk of pipe into his duffel bag. He also tossed in a compass, a lighter, a pair of wool socks, leather gloves, and a small video camera. The bag contained two high-protein bars and a sack of mixed nuts too—this adventure would require strength and endurance.

Before closing the bag, Tom reached in one last time and wrapped his fingers around the heavy ten-inch galvanized pipe. The weapon, measuring two inches in diameter, felt good in his hands. The cement that filled its center gave the pipe just the right amount of heft to do some serious damage to a man's skull. That thought made him smile. He tucked it under the socks and closed the bag.

As he hoisted the bag from the floor to his shoulder, Tom's dad, Carl Huffmann, entered the garage. The son could feel his father's presence. Tension swept across Tom's body. His stomach tightened, knotting—almost making the younger man ill.

"Let's get a move on, Tom. Time is a-wasting," Carl said, making for the workbench to pack his own supplies for the Saturday outdoor adventure.

Tom did not respond. Instead he grabbed his bag and carried it out to the pickup truck, dumping it into the back of the crew cab with the half-dozen other bags containing the cold-weather and fishing gear they'd packed earlier. It landed on the floor with a thud.

Carl and Tom, separated in age, thinking, and outlook by forty years, had never been particularly close. Tom was the youngest of Carl's three sons. The two older Huffmann boys had moved off the family's Huron County farm right after high school graduation, eager to say good-bye to the hardheaded and abusive old man as soon as they could.

The only Huffmann daughter, Katie, was the youngest member of the clan and Tom's stepsister. For the most part, Katie had escaped her stepdad's wrath and heavy hand. "Princess" was her nickname in the family. "Bitch" is what they called her at Laker High School.

Betty, Carl's second wife, hovered over Katie like a hen protecting her chicks. She left the upbringing of her stepson, Tom, to Carl and his belt.

As the two men climbed into the pickup truck, Carl tried to set the agenda for the day's events. Always, the older man took control.

"I was kinda hoping we could patch things up some," the aging farmer said, opening his tobacco pouch and nabbing a pinch of dark, stringy chaw to place between his cheek and teeth. He watched his son warily, as though he was looking for some kind of acknowledgment that Tom would try to make this a good trip. "You know, have some fun out on the bay, ice fishing and shooting the breeze—like we did when you were a kid."

Tom did not look at his father. He had his own plans for their afternoon on Saginaw Bay, and they didn't involve having fun or mending fences. What he had in mind would change his life—and his family's future—forever. "Sure, Dad. Whatever you say."

The older man pulled the Chevy out of the cavernous garage and headed down the driveway, which snaked more than a half mile across the family spread to the main road. Both men looked out their side windows without speaking. A low, steady growl from the truck's laboring heater was the only sound in the cab. The vehicle did not have a radio because the family patriarch had deemed such a contraption a frivolous luxury.

Tom recalled one of his old man's favorite sayings: "You want music? Hum a few bars from the hymns at Sunday service." The truck also featured hand-crank windows, a stick shift, and manual door locks. The floor mats were vinyl, as were the seat covers.

They passed by acres of flat farmland, now frozen by the harsh winds and plunging temperatures that were not uncommon for December in Michigan. The Huffmann family farm, nearly two thousand acres of prime Saginaw Valley soil, stretched as far as they could see—and then some. The homestead was everything to the Huffmanns. Carl saw it as his family's legacy, something worth protecting and passing on. Tom saw it as a cash cow and longed for the day he could claim it as his own.

As they drove north toward Saginaw Bay, churning wind turbines stood out against the cloud-filled sky. Tom could not resist the opportunity to get a dig in at his dad. "You see that, Pops?" A grin spread across his face. "That's money twirling around out there in those fields, and everybody is getting it but us."

The older man wet his lips. "Looks more like giant monsters swatting at birds, destroying our land," he said, pausing to let the remark settle on his son. He picked up an empty coffee cup from the floor of the truck cab and drizzled tobacco juice from his lips into the container. "More to life than money. Got to protect the family farm—the land, Tom. It's always about the land. You'll see that one day."

Tom shook his head, trying to understand his old man's thinking but not caring what he had to say, particularly about the wind turbines.

The two did not speak again until the pickup hit a pothole in the road. One of the 4-wheelers parked atop the trailer they were pulling bounced and landed off-center, shifting the load.

Carl looked at his son and shook his head.

"What?" Tom asked.

"Can't I count on you to do anything right?" Carl brought the pickup to a halt on the side of the road. "I asked you to secure those 4-wheelers, a small task that you just couldn't seem to get done." He slid out of the cab to check the machine.

Tom stayed where he was. He did not respond, but he boiled inside, looking out the passenger's side window, his fists clenched like a workbench vise. His jaw was so tight, his molars hurt. Tom's heartbeat quickened, and he began to snort in abrupt blasts. He wanted to throttle his old man, but he calmed himself, figuring that his dad's time was coming.

When Carl hopped back into the cab, he reported that one of the tie-down straps had snapped, probably from the shift in weight when the trailer hit the pothole. He said nothing else, putting the truck in gear and continuing down the road.

Tom waited for the apology that he knew would never come; his old man was never wrong, so there was never a need to say sorry for anything he'd done. Usually Tom let it slide and absorbed the sharp edges of the cutting remarks. But today he could not let it go. He simmered with rage for what seemed like forever but was really no more than five minutes. Then finally a river of emotions spilled out.

The younger man shifted in his seat to confront his father. "So, I guess what you're saying—without saying it—is that the 4-wheeler bouncing around in the back was not my fault after all. Is that right?"

Carl continued driving, looking straight ahead. "I said the strap broke," he replied in an even tone.

"Yes, but you implied that the 4-wheeler bouncing around was my fault," Tom said. "That you couldn't count on me. That I couldn't do anything right." Spit flew from his lips and landed on his dad's right shirt-sleeve.

Carl noticed the flying spittle out of the corner of his eye, but he chose to ignore it. "You can interpret what I said any way you want," his father told him. "I didn't come out here to get into an argument with you. I'd hoped we'd enjoy ourselves today. Have some fun, not fight."

"If you want to have fun, then quit being such an asshole," Tom said. "Why do you have to be a nasty jerk all the time? That's why my brothers are gone. That's why your new wife hardly talks to you anymore. That's why Katie stays away from you too."

Silence filled the cab once again. Tension. Anger. Frustration. Feelings that Tom always seemed to have when he was anywhere near his dad.

The two turned onto Filion Road, and before long Mud Creek came into view. The Mud was a shallow, dirty tributary that fed Saginaw Bay. As they neared the landing and launch area, they saw ice fishermen scrambling to gather their gear for a day out on the bay.

Sudden doubt raced across Carl's mind. He wondered if this outing was a big mistake. The divide between father and son just might be too wide for him to bridge, he thought, and he wasn't sure their relationship could ever be repaired. But he knew accidents happened out on the big lake—in summer and during the winter.

The older man pulled into the state water access site and parked the truck and trailer near the boat launch. Within minutes the two would be rolling out onto the frozen bay, searching for perch and walleye. Both men scanned the ice on Wild Fowl Bay, looking for clear, open areas to fish. Both wanted to be out of sight. And both would be looking for a place to bring a miserable life to an end.

Chapter 2

As reporters rolled into the newsroom of *The Bay City Blade* on Saturday morning, they spotted an unfamiliar sight. Nick Steele, veteran reporter and sometime wayward party hound, was slumped in his chair with his head on his desk. Snores came in short bursts with long, whooshing exhales. He wore the same rumpled and stained clothes from the day before—a tired blue sports jacket, wrinkled slacks that once were tan, and a misbuttoned dress shirt, revealing a T-shirt left over from a Tom Petty concert.

Nick's colleagues, an assortment of malcontents, misfits, and hopeless dreamers, checked in for their assignments and then hovered around the sleeping reporter's desk. One whispered, "Do you think he's still drunk?"

"Could be. See how his notebook is soaking up drool?"

"I'm not brave enough to see if he soiled himself."

A third reporter, almost giggling like an eighth-grader, suggested that this might be a good time to prank Nick. "I'll run down to the cafeteria and get some catsup. We squirt some in his hand, then tickle the side of his face with a feather."

The suggestion drew a round of muffled laughter from the group gathering around Nick's desk. Most liked and respected Nick Steele because of his dedication to their profession and the volume of top-notch work he produced. But others, particularly those who were often viewed as too casual about their craft, did not care for Nick's lack of patience and short temper. The latter group was winning this discussion.

Before a catsup bottle could be fetched, the frivolity dissipated like air coming out of a crunched lunch bag. Drayton Clapper, *The Blade's* managing editor, had a knack for taking the hoop out of the hoopla.

"All right, all right, you bunch of hyenas. Break it up and get me some copy. We got a newspaper to get out," he said, scowling as the reporters scattered like mice from the range of a hungry cat. Clapper was respectfully referred to as the C-Man. This was his domain. "Leave the guy alone. Nick was here all night working on a piece for Sunday's paper. He's wiped out."

Clapper, shaped like a miniature sumo wrestler, headed toward Nick's desk with the longest strides his stocky legs could make. Reporters dove into their notebooks or began pounding their computer keyboards. The pace quickened, and the newsroom soon zipped with activity.

The Blade, a small daily covering Up North Michigan in a triangle running from Bay City to the Mackinac Bridge and across to Bad Axe in the Thumb, served about forty-five thousand readers. The newsroom staff numbered fifty, including reporters, photographers, editors, designers, and clerks. The *Blade* team was tight and versatile, able to switch gears and cover just about any news story that came up on their radar.

Now, with the clatter of keys and hum of phone calls, mixed with a smattering of griping and whispered gossip, Nick's stutter-like snore seemed completely out of place. Clapper reached down and gently shook the reporter's shoulder. "Nick, hey, time to go home. You gotta get some real rest."

A voice from the back announced Nick's rise: "He's alive! He's actually moving! Better call O'Hare's and tell them to breathe easy—they're not going to lose their best customer yet."

Slowly the reporter emerged from a deep slumber. Clapper gave him a second, easier shake.

As he did, a reporter with horn-rimmed glasses boomed from a corner, "I'm still betting Nick finished his piece about eleven, then went to a pub and drank the bar dry."

Every newsroom has its cynics, critics, and smartasses, but *The Blade* seemed to be overly blessed with its share these days. Before anyone responded to the slam, Nick stood up at his desk. What time was it, he wanted to know.

"Still early, Nick. You got time to get some sleep before your interview this afternoon," C-Man said, looking up at the newsroom deadline clock. Nick didn't have to be out on Sand Point until about four, he said.

Horn-rims asked out loud how come Nick got a travel assignment to one of the most beautiful places on earth, while he was stuck covering a group of Santa Claus Salvation Army bell-ringers whose claim to fame was that they stood outside the mall and rapped Christmas carols hip-hop style.

Nick was already gathering his notebooks and gear. "Because the source called me," he said. "She asked if I would come out to interview her. I ran the whole idea by the C-Man, and he set the appointment for me."

That took the steam out of the inquiry. Nick headed for the exit sign at the back of the newsroom. He had lots to do before his late-afternoon interview, and he was looking forward to the hour-long ride out to the Thumb. His instincts told him this was going to be another good story.

Chapter 3

Nora Thompson opened the trunk of her car and poked through the boxes of decorations. She hoped her daughters had packed the praying angel that, as always, would adorn the top of a ten-foot blue spruce. This Christmas would be the first time in at least ten years that the Thompsons would celebrate the holiday at their cabin on the south shore of Sand Point, a peninsula that juts four miles out into Saginaw Bay. Today had been declared Decoration Day, the date in early December when the family would start getting the place ready for the holiday gathering.

Nora, a tiny woman with short graying hair, hefted a box almost as long as she was tall. It was loaded with strings of Christmas lights for the large Michigan white pine that reached forty feet into the sky on the lakeside of the cottage. Attaching the lights to the monster tree would be a task for her sons to tackle with the help of a tall ladder and their dad before the sun set later that afternoon.

Nora put the box on the picnic table and looked out at the lake, frozen from the shoreline out to several miles past North Island. Ice fishermen with small outhouse-style shanties and assorted gear dotted the ice like ants scrambling across a powder-blue plate. This view was beautiful and peaceful, she thought, no matter what time of year.

The cottage, a two-story chalet with chocolate-brown cedar siding on the outside and varnished knotty pine gracing the inside walls, had been in the family for almost fifty years. Its first owners were Nora's parents. Her fondest childhood memories could be found among the tall, whispering pines and the rocks scattered along the shoreline. This was her comfort zone, the place where the whole family could escape from the craziness of big-city life.

Nora considered sitting down on a nearby fire pit bench to enjoy the solitude and postcard view for a while, but decided against it because of the duties at hand. When she heard her daughters squabbling about the chores from inside the cottage, it sealed the deal. She would referee, separate them, and then start directing the work crew. A retired registered nurse, Nora was used to giving orders and making sure they were followed.

"Knock it off, you two," she said, striding toward the cottage. "We've got a ton of work to do before your dad gets here."

The young women, though in their early twenties, did not argue. They knew better.

Sarah, who sported enough flesh ink to publish a daily edition of the *Detroit Free Press*, as her dad liked to say, was assigned the bedrooms. These needed dusting from top to bottom, window cleaning, a date with the cabin's Hoover, and fresh bed linens.

Natasha pulled the short straw for this visit. She was given bathroom duty: wipe the tile from the ceiling down, scour the tubs and showers, scrub the windows and sinks, and re-introduce a hard-bristle brush to the toilets. If it didn't smell like chlorine, then it still wasn't clean, at least according to her mom.

Natasha squawked about her assignment. "How come I always get the shit-house jobs? I mean, come on. It's because dad doesn't like my piercings, right?"

It was true that her father despised the hardware in her face, ears, and neck. He often teased her that she looked like she'd fallen face down into a fishing tackle box, a comment that infuriated Tash. But what she didn't acknowledge was that her dad was equally critical of Sarah's tattoos, suggesting that her desire for tats had driven up the cost of ink all across the nation.

Usually Nora let the biting remarks pass with only a cursory verbal swat at Gary, her husband of thirty-two years. She knew he loved his girls and meant well. Occasionally she pushed him to change tactics, but it was tough because of the cultural divide in the family.

The young women carped at each other again, but their mom did not intervene. She was busy.

Nora's own cabin assignment, as always, included bringing the kitchen to order and getting dinner started. These tasks also allowed her to keep an eye on her daughters while prodding them along. "Let's keep it moving, girls. When you're done, I expect to see you converge on the living and dining rooms with reckless abandon. They're filthy."

The place had to be squeaky clean by the time a special guest arrived at the family cottage late in the afternoon. Nora had scheduled an interview with noted news reporter Nick Steele of *The Bay City Blade*.

The retired nurse had rejected three earlier requests from the paper but finally had consented when the editor of *The Blade* called and assured her that Steele would conduct the interview and write the story himself. The woman, who had been called Nice Nurse Nora for years by fellow practitioners because of the way she gently handled patients, was not a publicity hound in any way. But Nora had been pulled into a national story because of something that had happened to her and her coworkers. After much prodding— careful personal reflection—she had decided to tell her side. But she would only do so if Steele, whom she knew by reputation, handled the job.

She looked out the living room's large picture window, which framed the lake, and thought about what she would say to the reporter. Storm clouds had gathered on the horizon across Saginaw Bay. If a shift in the weather was coming, she wished it would roll in after her husband arrived at the cottage. Already the engineer was running late.

Later, when Gary came with the boys, the fireplace and grill would be cleaned and fired up. Then they would hang the Christmas tree lights outside, hopefully before night crept up on them around five o'clock. After the lights were up, they would turn on holiday music, prepare a meal, wrap gifts, and decorate the family tree. No TVs, no cell phones, no laptops or internet. It was an evening the whole family looked forward to enjoying together.

But before family time came, Nora had to get through the interview that she had promised to give. She looked out the picture window again as shadows fell across the horizon. Her arms were crossed over her bosom. Her fingers drummed her upper arms. She wanted it to come off well, and she hoped the reporter would be impressed with her family and their refuge on Sand Point.

Chapter 4

Jay-Bob Ratchett swung open the side door of the Huron County Sheriff's Department office and dropped a box of court records in the hallway leading to the jail.

"Hey, don't anybody give me a gol-durned hand with this stuff," he said. Dead silence.

The hall was empty. The walls were bare. By the way it looked, the local hardware store must have had a sale on beige paint. Light brown covered the walls and ceilings, giving the inside of the building a dingy look. Bland was too colorful a word to describe it.

Distant, muffled shouts from the county jail, located down the passageway in an adjacent building, rattled through the tunnel-shaped hall. In the reception area between the two, a lone deputy was assigned to handle incoming calls and work the front window.

In one not-so-smooth motion, Jay-Bob pushed the overflowing box further into the hall with his boot and pulled the door closed with his arm. "Where in the hell is everybody?" he said, moving toward the deputy's overflowing desk. Again, no response from the deputy on duty, who was busy taking care of personal business, dispatching her credit card bill and house and car payments while Jay-Bob rattled on about getting in the door.

Ratchett, whose birth name was James Robert, had been known as Jay-Bob since he quarterbacked the Bad Axe Hatchets football team in high school. The shortened version was better than his childhood nickname, Booger, which he had been tagged with because of his penchant for having at least one finger up a tunnel to his sinuses all day. His friends were merciless and accused him of packing his lunch in his nose.

Booger's coach, Rich Jeric, had tried to change the teen's nickname because it was used derisively by his teammates. The veteran coach started calling his signal caller "Ace," but the players piled on, turning the new moniker into "Ass." Unfortunately, "Ace" never stuck. Contrived nicknames seldom do.

Nicknames were common in a rural, heartland town like Bad Axe, a city of 1,500 and the seat of local government for Huron County. It was the hub of activity for social groups, economic discussions, and political discourse in the county, but it was also a place where the big entertainment for the week might be the Friday night football game or a selection from a wide assortment of church fairs.

When the position of detective-sergeant came open in the sheriff's department, Jay-Bob was the only applicant. He proudly took the job, and he did his best to uphold the law and serve residents. But crime did not run rampant in the county—mostly petty theft, traffic offenses, some drug activity, and drunk driving. Not a lot of demand for serious crime-solving, so Jay-Bob found himself shuffling records between court, the prosecutor's office, and the jail. Jay-Bob did the work—but not without making it known that a man of his immense talent should not be wasting his skills lugging around boxes of paper.

Jay-Bob left the records in the hall and sauntered into the reception area. The deputy behind the glass rolled her eyes, waiting on an elderly man who wanted to leave some spending money in an inmate account. The officer, a short, stocky woman with long black hair pulled into a ponytail, told the man she didn't have time to print out a receipt for him. She asked him to come back tomorrow.

"I can't wait or come back," he said, explaining that his wife was waiting for him in a cold pickup truck outside. "Can I just leave it with you?"

Ponytail nodded. Her hair, bound with a thick rubber band that had probably been used to hold broccoli stalks together, flopped up and down against the back of her neck. The old man expressed his thanks, handed over an envelope, and shuffled to the door.

After he had walked away from the building, Ponytail tore open the envelope and put the cash in her side desk drawer. Jay-Bob watched as the empty envelope landed in the trash.

"You know, I should turn you in for that," he said, pointing at the basket with his chin. "That's the biggest crime we've had this week. Stealing from the poor and disadvantaged—why, it's just not right. You should be locked up in the back with the animals."

"The money would have ended up in the hands of a drug dealer," she said, laughing loudly enough to frighten the birds sitting on a ledge outside the office window. "He ain't going to miss it, and nobody will ever know because the surveillance camera is down right now. So mind your own business, Jay-Bob, and everything will be fine—same as always. Go be a detective somewhere else."

Jay-Bob grunted his disapproval, moving past her into the empty office area. He asked where all the other deputies were hiding on a Saturday afternoon.

Ponytail said that the wind on the lake had shifted. Warm breezes were coming in from the northeast, melting ice on the bays and inlets. Ice fishermen working the shallows and protected areas would find themselves stranded on floes or breaking through the mushy ice.

Her fellow deputies, who also comprised the department's marine unit and water-rescue squad, were busy scrambling along the shoreline, urging ice fishermen to protect themselves and come ashore. But folks who spent their free time angling were largely an independent lot, and they rarely paid attention to such warnings. When answering a call for them to abandon their holes in the ice, they were more likely to respond with a raised middle finger than heed a call for reason and prudence.

Jay-Bob retrieved his messages from his desk and noted the top one, which urged him to return the call right away. It was signed with the initials BH. He stuffed it into the pants pocket of his uniform.

Ponytail scooted to the ladies' room. Jay-Bob waited for the door to close, then walked back to her desk. He pulled the cash out of her desk drawer and put it in his pocket.

"Ain't right to steal from someone locked up," he said out loud. "But stealing from a thief, well, that's just karma."

The deputy whistled as he headed for his white, black, and gold patrol car.

Chapter 5

Tom and Carl Huffmann dressed in their cold-weather gear as quickly as they could inside the tight, cramped space of the pickup truck cab. Insulated everything—snowmobile suits, mittens, boots, and big furry hats with tie-down earflaps—ruled the day for many out on the ice. Bright hunter's orange, designed for maximum visibility, was the color of choice for everything, including their socks. Carl's only deviation from orange garb was a bright-blue scarf, a gift from his loving wife.

The afternoon was slipping away from them. The two only had about three hours of good light left in the day. Tom did not want to miss the opportunity to get his dad alone with him on the ice. The older man was still hoping to rekindle their relationship, or end it abruptly. They hustled out into the cold and steered their quad runners toward what was commonly known as the Slot on Wild Fowl Bay.

The Slot was a ridge located about halfway between the end of Sand Point and the northern edge of North Island, where the lake depth dropped suddenly from about four feet to almost ten. Anglers loved to fish on both sides of the Slot because their prey often fed there. The area allowed men and women on the ice to haul fish from the depths of the lake like felines clawing delights out of tuna cans.

Today's weather had turned out to be perfect for ice fishing. Warm sunshine poked through a partly cloudy sky, with temperatures hovering in the high twenties. Winds were light but gusty as the Huffmann guys bounced along the ice on their machines. Tom's quad pulled their sled, which carried a portable shanty and gear.

The two stopped frequently to chat with the canaries, anglers who were called that because they had been out fishing near the edge of safe ice—lookouts for danger, just like the canaries in coal mining days. All reports indicated that the ice was solid, with a good six to eight inches of thickness well past the Slot.

The recent cold snap had frozen Wild Fowl Bay from its base at Bay Port to North Island, a distance of about 3.5 miles. Further past North Island, however, the water depth varied wildly, depending on the location of shifting sand bars. But the deeper the water, the thinner the ice. Lake Huron, except along its shoreline, was still open water.

Carl slowed his machine when he spotted Jon Barrett coming out of his ice shanty not far from the Slot. About two dozen twelve-inch perch, their gills billowing feverishly for air, flopped on a mound of snow near the shanty. The coughing engines of the 4-wheelers drowned the two men's voices, but Tom leaned toward them, trying to pick up on the conversation. Whatever the avid outdoorsman had to share, Tom Huffmann wanted to hear it.

Most folks in Huron County knew of the wild adventure that had made Jon Barrett a legend throughout the area just a few years before. The local newspapers, including *The Bay City Blade*, had carried detailed articles about the ice-capade.

Barrett and his father had been ice fishing on a relatively warm day off the north shore of Sand Point when they suddenly discovered that the surface they were standing on had broken off from the main ice shelf. The two men, along with dozens of others, were stranded on an ice floe that was shrinking and drifting at a frightening rate.

No rescuers were in sight. Jon Barrett had sized up the situation and jumped into the frigid water himself—nearly six feet deep at that point. Moving continuously in the cold, Jon swam and waded more than one hundred yards to safe ice.

Once on shore, he hurried to his dad's lakefront cottage, changed clothes, and then launched the family's aluminum fishing boat, maneuvering the small craft between chunks of floating ice and out toward the ice floe in open water. By then it had drifted more than a thousand yards from the ice shelf near shore.

Jon helped his dad climb aboard the boat and took him to safety. But the job at hand was not complete; he and three other local men, Mike Quinn, Bob Adams, and Al Eicher, made several more runs out to the melting ice floe. When they finished just before dark, twenty-six ice anglers had been rescued.

As Tom recalled the story, which had been recounted in the media and in numerous coffee klatches, he couldn't help wondering how his life might have been different if he had grown up with a man like Jon Barrett for a dad. Instead Tom walked in the shadow of an uncompromising tyrant he had grown to despise.

Carl had finished talking to Barrett; he motioned for Tom to follow. The younger Huffmann waved at the man he admired and tagged along behind the man he loathed.

The Huffmanns first decided to try their luck in an open area where fishing holes had not yet been drilled that day. However, it was not an ideal spot for what Tom had in mind. Too many other anglers were visible out on the ice, and within shouting distance.

The men had barely started fishing when they began squabbling again. Carl had spotted the spinning wind turbines off in the distance, and the sight of them revved his inner engine. "No matter where you go in the county, you just can't get away from the damn things," he said, spitting a dark, thick stream of tobacco juice onto the ice and just missing Tom's boot. "It pisses me off that we let those monsters in our county and onto our farmland. I'd turn my back to them, but then I'd be sitting into the wind."

Tom shook his head and pulled his boot back out of range. He stared into the hole in front of him, trying to decide if he wanted to engage his old man in this debate yet another time. "When are you going to give it up? It's called progress, the future. They're here to stay, and we're missing out by not having them on our place. That's easy money we're not getting."

"Never going to happen as long as I'm drawing air."

Tom did not reply. He was not surprised by the response. He figured that Carl was right; there was only one way the wind turbine dispute would be settled between them, and he aimed to get it started today.

"No action here," Tom said. Let's try another spot."

The older man, still in a contrary humor, resisted, so the squabbling continued—long distance—as the two men fished over separate holes, with their backs to each other, about a hundred yards apart.

A snowmobile approached their setup, moving toward Carl. Tom did not pay much attention to it, though he noticed the driver, dressed in a navy blue snowmobile suit with a fur-lined hood and wearing sunglasses. Light-tan leather work gloves dangled from a hip pocket. The man got off the sled.

The two men talked, but Tom could not hear them because the snowmobile was left running. He sat upright when the talk turned to shoving as the two men jostled with each other near the fishing hole.

But a fourteen-inch perch nipped at Tom's bait, holding his attention. When it skittered away, he looked up again to see the two men wrestling with each other on the ice. That struck him as odd, but it didn't surprise him; his old man was always tussling with somebody. Carl Huffmann swung his right fist at the man beneath him. The wild swing made the older man lose his balance and the snowmobiler rolled him over on his back, reversing their positions.

Tom watched the two men separate, still yelling obscenities at each other. As the younger Huffmann stood up, the snowmobile driver shook his fist at Carl, cursed again, and got back on his machine.

"What was that all about?" Tom shouted, pulling his fishing gear together and hauling it in the direction of his dad.

Carl was covered in snow, his breathing labored. "Jerk claimed we jumped his fishing hole. Told him he was nuts. The SOB had been drinking—I could smell the whiskey when we were rolling on the ice. He said he'd get even. That'll be the day."

"You should have just told him to take it," Tom said. "We're not hitting much here anyway. Let's move on to deeper water."

Carl continued muttering about the snowmobiler as he collected himself and his gear. "I've heard of road rage before, but I've never seen ice rage. Hope I don't run across that asshole again."

"I want to catch some big fish. Let's get way out," Tom said. He also knew that the further out the two men went, the less likely they'd run into other anglers—or witnesses.

They loaded their gear and pointed their quads toward North Island. Dodging abandoned ice-fishing holes and numerous pressure cracks in the ice, the two made their way out toward the big water.

Chapter 6

Nick Steele pulled his gold 1967 Firebird out onto Bay City's legendary Center Avenue and directed the rumbling beast east toward the Thumb of Michigan, home to great farmland, fabulous Lake Huron coastline, and enough Republicans to give Rush Limbaugh a continuous stiffy.

The reporter took a deep breath and exhaled slowly, watching the city view fade into farmland. Fatigue from the package of stories he had just developed had overwhelmed him. He needed a break and a change of scenery. This trip would be especially pleasing, he thought, because he was heading into very familiar and comfortable territory.

Thumb farm country was where Nick had grown up. His family had run a small-time cattle operation and a two hundred-acre farm that produced enough crops to feed their livestock and the open market. Nick's dad had managed the farm while working full-time in the mobile home factories in Marlette. Later he'd taken a job with an automotive supplier in Sebewaing. Nick worked the farm with his pop while attending a small school in the country and played every sport that was available—baseball, basketball, and track, and football when the school had enough healthy kids to put a viable team on the gridiron.

Like a lot of families in the Thumb, the Steele clan had worked multiple jobs, often running at full speed from sun-up to dusk. When they were able to scrape together time for retreat, they spent every moment they could enjoying the sandy beaches, warm summer breezes, and rolling waves of the Caseville area. The family loved camping at Sleeper State Park. Campgrounds were set up for those who agreed there was nothing quite like a roaring campfire at sunset under a canopy of tall oaks.

These fond memories danced in Nick's head as he drove through the wide-open spaces. Field after field of harvested corn and sugar beets flashed by in the periphery. In among the traditional crops that ruled the huge, flat farm fields of the Thumb, more than four hundred wind turbines, their giant blades twirling five hundred feet in the air, churned out electrical power for the grid.

Wind turbines had become a source of controversy and conflict throughout the Thumb. Their rise across the horizon split communities, local governments, neighbors, and even families. Either you loved the sky scratchers or you hated them. Some folks in the county viewed turbines as part of the future as Michigan and the nation turned toward clean energy. Other citizens saw the turbines as a desecration of the heartland, humongous mechanical structures that destroyed scenic farm vistas, whacked birds out of the sky, and threatened farm life.

The debate had become so heated in some communities that elected officials had been threatened with bodily harm. At an open forum in Meade Township, a member of the farm community had suggested that Planning Commission members who favored the turbines should be taken out into the parking lot and horsewhipped.

Cooler heads generally prevailed, and only a handful of violent acts had actually been reported while the turbines were put into operation. The structures were built to generate power for twenty years and each cost $3.5 million to erect, so once they were up, they were there to stay.

Community leaders had rejected the idea of building turbines along the Saginaw Bay or Lake Huron shoreline—either in or out of the water. Nick was thankful for that, viewing it as an uncommon display of common sense by local government. He did not mind the turbines personally, but he did not have to live with them every day either.

Caseville had not changed much from Nick's childhood recollection of the area. Except for a handful of weeks in the summer, it was still a sleepy little resort town huddled around the mouth of the Pigeon River. Many of the town's eight hundred full-time residents were retirees, and most businesses shut down for the winter. Tourism was the economic engine for the community, with the annual Jimmy Buffet–themed Cheeseburger festival throwing Caseville into overdrive.

Caseville was very much like *Mayberry R.F.D.*, except that the town drunks did not lock themselves up in the local jail at night. Otherwise the similarities were eerie. But a small town is not a bad thing and can end up being wondrous. Each year in Caseville, for example, a handful of volunteers conducted a campaign to make sure every local child had a gift and a winter coat and boots for Christmas. It was said that you were only a stranger in Caseville if you wanted to be one.

As Nick passed through the tiny fishing village of Bay Port, he thought about the interview with Nora and where the story with her might go.

Nora Thompson, in his book, was a courageous woman. She was now ready to speak out against the thug-like tactics of the US government that she had experienced several years earlier while working as a nurse for a home health care agency in the Thumb.

The agency, which had served about three hundred patients in a wide oval from Bad Axe to Midland, was apparently too efficient and successful; it became a government target for suspected Medicare fraud.

From what Nick had learned of the tale, Nora and a handful of other health care specialists were just getting their day started at the agency's headquarters in Pigeon early on a Monday morning, when the office was stormed by forty federal agents, wearing protective vests and wielding pistols and stun guns.

"Everyone step away from your desks. Do not touch anything or say anything until you are spoken to," the commander barked. His raid team fanned out around him, surveying the offices, their occupants, and their contents. Armed with a federal search warrant, the agents loaded up and hauled away all the agency's paper files and copied the contents of the company's computer files.

The incident had horrified the agency's employees and patients and shocked the small farming community of Pigeon. No one had ever seen that many federal agents— accompanied by reporters from three TV and radio stations—in town. The raid, particularly the force and long reach of the government, was the talk of Huron County for weeks.

Nora, who had been a health care professional for more than two decades, was so stunned by the incident that she had quit nursing and refused to talk about it with associates or friends. It was only when she was assured Nick Steele would conduct her interview that she agreed to reveal her side of the story.

Nick had told her he looked forward to the opportunity to work on the story. He had not done much writing about the so-called heavy-handed tactics of the federal government, and he hoped to focus his reporting on how the raid had changed the lives of the people—both patients and employees of the company—involved.

The reporter turned off M-25 and onto Crescent Beach Road, heading due west on Sand Point, which had become a haven for well-heeled senior citizens. Many of the old-timers on Sand Point had held executive positions in the auto industry or in private business. Some were bankers, lawyers, investors, inventors, entrepreneurs, or high-level educators. Dwellings ranged from cottages to year-round homes to mansions that might be noted in a glossy magazine article entitled "Homes of the Filthy Rich & Wish-They-Weres."

The Thompson place soon came into Nick's view. Its homey charm and serene setting caught him by surprise. Lights glowed from every room inside the cedar chalet. Why were all the truly fabulous places located at what seemed like the ends of the earth? he asked himself, pausing to soak up the view like a dry sponge exposed to water.

While in the driveway, Nick spotted three men putting up Christmas tree lights on a giant pine near the lakeshore. They stopped long enough to wave the reporter up toward the lakeside of the cottage, which was built on a sand ridge just two hundred feet from the water's edge.

Nick stood next to the walkway and scanned the horizon. Small clusters of ice fishermen moved about on the frozen water. Dark, bulging clouds, stacked like fluffy pillows, filled the sky. A warm breeze from the northeast hit the side of Nick's face.

His trance was broken by the sound of Nora Thompson's voice. She and her daughters had come out to greet Nick. They introduced themselves, then took Nick to the side of the property where her husband, Gary, and sons, Ted and Richard, wrestled with a huge wad of Christmas tree lights.

"They'll join us inside when they get finished up," Nora said, leading the way to the roadside entrance to the house. "Shouldn't take too long. I'm ready to get going on the interview when you are."

Chapter 7

Jay-Bob Ratchett slowed his patrol car to a crawl. An old John Deere tractor weaved all over the state highway, veering wildly from one side to the other at about ten miles per hour.

The deputy recognized the driver as an old schoolmate who'd fallen on hard times and turned to the sauce for solace. Jay-Bob did not want to add to his old friend's woes, but he had to get the guy off the road. He flicked the switch for the flashers. Raging red and blue lights danced across snow-covered State Park Road, illuminating the area as darkness fell like a shade being pulled over a window.

The tractor continued down the road in the same zig-zag fashion.

Next Jay-Bob tried the cruiser's siren, opening it up to eardrum-shattering level. The tractor driver did not turn around; nor did he seem to notice he was being followed. Finally the deputy timed the zig and zag to zip out around the farm machine. The passing maneuver shot Jay-Bob ahead of his buddy, where he blocked the roadway with his cruiser, lights flashing and siren still screaming.

A smile crossed the tractor driver's face, which was crimson from the sharp, cool wind. Dale Fickbeiner pulled the tractor to the side of the road and shut off its engine. He jumped off the machine, his stocky frame bouncing, or perhaps staggering, sideways against the huge tractor wheel.

"Hey, Booger, what's you up to?" he asked with a genuinely quizzical look. Dale wore greasy brown coveralls with a red hooded sweatshirt underneath. His black leather boots were ringed at the bottom in cow manure. Thick, fingerless mittens protected his hands from the cold. He waved the right one at his old friend and nodded uneasily.

Light lake-effect snow fluttered in the breeze coming from Lake Huron. The white stuff filled the air, quickly accumulating on the shoulders of the two old friends as they faced each other in a very uncomfortable situation.

"Hey, Dale. What the gol-durned heck are you doing out here?" Jay-Bob asked, ignoring Dale's use of his childhood name. "You know you ain't supposed to drive drunk—whether it's a car, a truck, or a tractor. You can't drive drunk on any public road."

"Aw, come on." The grin had fallen off Dale's face. "I only had a couple of belts for lunch after pitching cow shit all mornin'. You seen me drunk before, and believe me, this ain't drunk."

"Doesn't matter, Dale. I'm going to have to give you a breathalyzer and run you in—that's all there is to it. No telling how many people have seen you out here driving crazy on this road. I got to do it, buddy. Sorry, but there's no way around it."

Dale's head slowly fell until his chin rested on his chest.

Jay-Bob opened his cruiser's rear door and motioned for Dale to take a seat. As he did, an alert blared across the car's radio: Some fishermen had broken through the ice on Lake Huron near the mouth of the Pinnebog River, not far from M-25. A rescue unit was on its way to the scene, but the dispatcher urged all available personnel to respond to the call for assistance.

Jay-Bob's face sagged. Some folks were in trouble out on the lake, but he had a snockered tractor driver standing before him. He knew he could not just leave the tractor on the side of the road for an unsuspecting motorist to run into at night. Right or wrong, Jay-Bob decided to act quickly.

The deputy placed Dale in the back of his patrol car for safe-keeping, but without arresting him. He then started the John Deere and drove it to the next farm field driveway, where he left it out of harm's way.

"Today is your lucky day," Jay-Bob said, gasping for air as he slid in behind the wheel of the cruiser. He turned to tell Dale that he would drive him home on his way to the lake.

But his old school chum did not respond. Dale sat slumped across the back seat, snoring like a tired hound dog. The morning's hard work, the brisk air outdoors, and whatever he'd had in his "couple of belts" at lunchtime had done him in for the day.

Jay-Bob dropped Dale at his place, about a mile away, in the care of his wife, Judy, who did not seem surprised at her hubby's condition—or impressed by it. As the deputy backed out of the driveway, he could hear Judy giving Dale, still passed out, holy hell.

"Now, that's what I call cruel and unusual punishment," Jay-Bob said. He pointed the patrol car in the direction of the Pinnebog River, his lights ablaze.

Chapter 8

Tom Huffmann fired up the gasoline-powered auger and drilled his sixth hole in the ice. Each hole was about a foot apart, forming a circle. Then he punched the center of the circle with the auger, and the ice caved into the water. He pushed the big chunk—ten inches thick—under the edge of the ice. "Just big enough for the old man's shoulders to clear," he muttered, congratulating himself on such a nice, clean job.

"Why'd you make the hole so big?" Carl asked as he brought their gear—fishing poles, a can of bait, and buckets to sit on—to the edge of the ice. "You figurin' to land a monster catfish or sturgeon?"

Tom felt the side of his parka for the chunk of cement-filled pipe he'd tucked into his belt. "Only want to drill once, so I made it plenty big." The pipe was in place and ready for use when needed.

Both men baited their lines and got them into the water. They sat on their buckets with their backs to the wind. The breeze had warmed and picked up. The fat clouds filling the sky had begun to part in the west, allowing the setting sun to scatter rays of bright light across parts of the lake.

Carl examined the hole again and noted to himself that it looked big enough even for Tom to go through easily. No other ice anglers were in sight, he noticed; they had called it a day and were loading up on shore. Carl scanned the shoreline. Most lakefront cottages had been closed up for the winter, their windows shuttered. No lights were on, and no smoke wafted from the chimneys. Except for the occasional whine from a snowmobile engine, it was dead quiet on the lake.

"Easy as pie," he muttered. He looked forward to the moment

when the biggest mistake and embarrassment of his life would be a sad memory.

As they jigged, or bounced their bait up and down in the water, Carl Huffmann recalled the first time they had gone ice fishing together. Tom was eight years old and had not liked sticking his hook into the belly of a shiner. "Doesn't it hurt when you jam 'em with that big hook?" Tom had asked.

Carl recounted the story now, laughing. "Do you remember asking me that?" he said.

Tom smiled. "Yup, and you said something like 'Fish don't have feelings like you and me.' I still didn't want to bait my hook, though. Mighty glad you did it for me."

The Huffmann men chuckled at the memory and talked more about their early fishing experiences. Tom described the time when he was in sixth grade and the two of them were ice fishing on the bay, and Carl's fishing rig—line, bait, and pole—were pulled into the hole and dragged away by a pissed-off pike.

Their banter was interrupted by a school of perch below. The men took turns hauling in twelve-inchers, just big enough to clean and make decent fillets. About a dozen fish were scattered on the ice, flopping alongside their buckets, occasionally hitting the sides of their seats.

Carl sipped his coffee and pulled in another big perch. "Wow, this turned out to be a good spot." The old man paused to pull out his pouch of chewing tobacco. He stuffed a wad in his cheek and held the pouch out for Tom, who, as usual, declined the opportunity to chew. "You wanna stay awhile or move before it gets dark?"

Tom shrugged; he was not in a hurry to move on. He had other ideas.

"Gotta stretch my legs," Tom said, watching his dad work the tobacco in the side of his mouth like a cow chewing her cud. He stood up from his bucket and circled behind his dad.

The wind picked up, blowing drifted snow from the north. It was stiff enough to flip over the Huffmanns' empty sled.

The younger man unzipped his parka. He reached inside and pulled out the pipe, raising it over his head.

Carl jigged his line and spat a light spray of tobacco juice just to the right of his fishing hole. He shifted the wad in his mouth to the other side and turned the conversation to the two men's deer hunting experiences. Tom's mom, Joyce, would sometimes join them when they were out near the edge of the woods sitting in blinds, hunting over bait piles. She had been with them when Tom bagged his first six-point buck.

"I know she loved hunting with us," Carl said. "Those were some of the happiest times of my life."

"Mine too," Tom said, lowering the pipe. "I miss Mom every day."

Joyce had filled both men's lives with, well, joy for as long as they could remember. But a car accident, which Carl blamed on Tom and Tom blamed on Carl, had taken her life.

While she was on her way to pick up young Tom from a friend's birthday party, the brakes on her car had failed, and she had veered off the dirt road and rammed a sturdy oak. The last person to service the brakes on the car was Carl, and the only reason she had driven that day was to retrieve Tom from his friend's place. Each blamed the other for the greatest loss in their lives.

That's when Tom had started despising his father. Everything his old man did after that had only added to the hatred.

Carl pulled out his handkerchief to blow his nose. Tom could see that his old man was weeping. The younger Huffmann put the pipe back in his belt inside the parka.

"Maybe you're right," Tom said. "Let's move before it gets dark.

I'd like to land some walleye. Freezer in the garage is getting a little low."

The two men loaded their gear onto the sled. Carl took the lead on his 4-wheeler as they headed west, toward North Island. Tom pulled up closer to his dad. He scanned the sky, noting how dusk seemed to be coming rapidly.

Popping noises like firecrackers muffled the roar of their machines. The older man held up his arm, a signal to stop. More popping, and the crashing of breaking ice. "Hightail it to shore now!" he screamed.

But it was too late. There was no escape. Nowhere to run. The lake reared up and swallowed the men and their machines.

Chapter 9

Nick sat down at the Thompsons' sturdy dining room table, which was built from reclaimed barn wood planks and finished with linseed oil. He admired the deep, swirling grain of the red oak. Some of the knotholes in the planking were big enough for Nick to probe with his pinky, but he resisted the urge to take the plunge.

Nice Nurse Nora placed a cup of steaming coffee in front of him and sat down across the table. Nick's notebook and pen were at the ready. He sipped at his coffee, stopping every few seconds to gently blow heat off the brew. He did not want to rush Nora; in his experience it was best to go slow when starting an interview, especially when seeking sensitive information from someone who was touchy about the subject.

"Love your place. I can see why you come here whenever you can," he said, hoping to warm Nora up with light conversation before they got started. He looked out the cottage's massive picture window, where dusk had fallen across Wild Fowl Bay.

"Thanks," she said with an easy sigh. "This is where we escape. Our professional lives are in the city—that's where the jobs are. But someday we hope to live here full-time because this is where our hearts and spirits are."

Nora was interrupted by the sound of the side door opening. Her husband, Gary, and their two sons burst through, stomping snow off their boots. "Done! Lights are up and the deck is swept off," Gary declared loudly enough for all inside the cottage to hear. "Best of all, the lights work—even after all these years sitting in a box."

Nick stood to meet the men. Tall and lean, with dark hair and deep-blue eyes, Gary had often been likened to Paul McCartney when he and the Beatles legend were both young. His two sons looked and stood just like their old man. The three guys were straight arrows— short, thick hair and clean-cut except for sideburns trimmed at the bottom of the ear. Their voices even sounded alike.

Nora conducted the introductions, telling each man a little about the other. Nick asked if he could go outside to see the newly lighted Christmas tree. Gary and the boys smiled with big, toothy grins. The Thompson daughters joined them from the kitchen, and they all went outside to get a good look at the massive tree.

By now darkness had descended on the lake. Forty feet of red, blue, white, and green teardrop-shaped lights gently shimmered in the warm wind off the bay.

The Thompson family stood on the outside deck, their arms draped around one another, smiling and admiring the view. The glowing tree was a sight to behold, but Nick was even more impressed by the closeness of the family and the pure joy they shared. Despite their differences, Nick believed this was a tight family. He envied the bonds they'd created. He had the feeling that if he looked over his shoulder, he might see a photo crew from Hallmark snapping off pictures for another classic Christmas season card.

Eventually the cold forced the group back inside the cottage. Nora directed Gary and the boys to the kitchen, where they were instructed to dive into the pot roast that had been simmering all afternoon, filling the cottage with the aroma of beef and light onion. The girls would join them when their chores were complete, and she and Nick would swoop in to polish off the dinner after their interview was finished and everyone could relax.

Nora joined Nick at the big oak table. He took it as a signal that she wanted to launch into the interview right away. He began by asking her why she had decided to talk about her experience now, more than three years after it happened.

The RN paused for a moment as her older daughter slid a plate of food in front of her. Nick looked at the plate. The portions were barely big enough to feed a bird.

"I'm more of a picker than a real eater," she said, noticing Nick's attention to the fare in front of her. "I eat a little here and there all day. It's been like that since I quit nursing."

Nick said he had heard she was going back into her profession. She nodded, nibbling on a carrot.

"Yes, I think I'm just about ready," she said, and looked down at her plate. The food had been pushed around but not consumed. "It's also the answer to your first question. I was so knocked off my feet by the government raid—and the aftermath—that I didn't even want to think about what happened, let alone talk about it publicly. Once the government dropped the case without bringing charges, I felt I had to speak up. So many people were hurt, so many affected. I know firsthand that it shattered lives. I'm ready to talk now."

Nora hesitated, getting teary. The cottage was silent. So was Nick.

After a few minutes Nora took a deep breath, but just as she opened her mouth to speak, the quiet was destroyed by a pounding at the lakeside door of the cottage. All eyes in the cottage shifted to the entrance.

Gary, who had been in the kitchen, moved to identify the source of the urgent thudding. Nick stood up from the table. Nora covered her gaping mouth. Sarah dropped her plate on the floor. The boys looked for their guns.

"Holy shit," Gary said as he flipped on the exterior lights and peered out the side window. "Somebody is out there." He opened the door slightly, blocking the bottom with his knee and boot. When his eyes adjusted to the shadowy light outside, he let the door swing open. A cold whoosh of air entered the cottage.

A large man leaned against the side of the doorframe, ice and snow covering the exposed area of his face. With his cold-weather gear frozen to his body, he looked like a giant popsicle. "We … need … help," he said, pleading and gulping for air. "My dad is still out there, still in the water. Help us, please."

Nick moved for the doorway, stunned by what he had witnessed and heard. Then he watched in awe as the RN took command.

"Guys, get him in here and out of those frozen clothes," she said. "Girls, we need blankets and towels—now. Nick, call 9-1-1. Everybody move, or get out of the way."

Chapter 10

As darkness fell across Lake Huron, Sheriff's Deputy Jay-Bob Ratchett opened the passenger's side door of his patrol car. A wave of glorious heat flowed into the face of his dripping wet temporary guest, Brad Prater.

Brad, who had been ice fishing near the mouth of the Pinnebog River just off Port Austin Road with nine other anglers, was glad to get out of the wind—and the water. He slid into the seat that the deputy had covered with a black plastic garbage bag.

"Thanks, Boog," Brad said. "I'd love to get out of this snowmobile suit, but my wife will be here shortly." He'd already summoned his wife via Jay-Bob's cell phone because his own was out there somewhere, probably the bottom of the lake.

Brad uncrossed his arms to let the warm air from the car's heater flow to his upper body. Water dripped from his frozen pant legs onto the floor mat of the cruiser. Beads of ice had formed on the outer edges of his full beard, and the sudden heat caused the ice to melt. Big droplets fell to his frozen collar. Long curls of matted brown hair dangled from the edges of his orange knit cap.

The tall, heavy angler filled the seat, and then some. His knees pushed against the top of the front dashboard as his labored breathing fogged the upper part of the windshield. Getting out of the lake had worn him out.

Jay-Bob pushed the vehicle door shut. He looked out over the lake. Already, paper-thin ice had formed where the anglers had broken through the frozen water. His new passenger was the last to get picked up; an ambulance had whisked away two of the fishermen, who had been completely submerged and had developed

42

chest pains.

Brad and the others were lucky, Jay-Bob knew. The water was only about waist deep where they had broken through the ice. They had lost their gear but were able to stand and pull themselves up on firm ice before waddling to shore like penguins.

Jay-Bob slid behind the wheel of his patrol car and let gravity close the door. He looked at his old high school friend, who was shivering in his wet clothes. "What in the gol-durned heck is wrong with you, Brad? Why in hell would you even go out on that ice with weather conditions changing like they did today?"

"Good fishin'—that's why, Boog!" he said, turning his head toward Jay-Bob without moving his cold body in the seat. "First and last ice is always the best to catch the big ones. You know that—you lived here your whole life."

"Yeah, yeah—but is it really worth risking your life for a few lousy fish?" Jay-Bob asked, his gloved hands resting on the steering wheel. "You can go to the Bay Port Fish Company and buy all the fish you want—cheap. I just don't get it. Why go out there and make the rescue crews come after you?"

Brad did not answer. He scanned the lake, his head slowly swiveling back and forth. Finally he looked at his old schoolmate. "Hey, I didn't fall in the lake on purpose," he said. "When we went out, it was solid. Then things changed, and we got in trouble. You came to help. That's your job. Quit whining about it."

The response riled Jay-Bob, who was cold and wet and tired. He tried to answer so quickly that he began to stutter and spit. "We-we-well, do-do-don't that be-be-beat all. Now you're telling me what my job is. Well, I ca-ca-can tell you one thing. Nowhere in my job description does it read: 'Be prepared to risk your life to go get morons off the ice when it begins to thaw.' Now, this time I didn't have to go out there to get you or any of your pals, but that's not how this usually plays out—and you know it."

Brad leaned back in his seat and took a deep breath. He lifted his right hand, still red from the cold, and brushed white flecks of the deputy's spittle from his coat sleeve. "Hey, Boog, I'm in no mood for a lecture right now, okay? Do you want me to wait outside for my wife to get here?"

Now Jay-Bob did not respond. Instead he reached into his jacket breast pocket and pulled out a flip cell phone that squawked for his attention. The deputy recognized the caller. He answered with one word—"Yup"—then listened intently, sitting upright in his seat. Then: "Okay, I'm on my way." He clicked off and stuck the cell back in his pocket.

"Brad, buddy, I got to fly," Jay-Bob said. "Since your wife ain't here, I'm going to run you to her. I'm heading for Sand Point. We'll go right by your place."

Jay-Bob turned his cruiser around and flicked the flashing lights on, heading toward Brad's place, which was near State Park Road, just off the main highway. The two men drove in silence. No words were necessary.

Chapter 11

Nick Steele picked up the chunk of pipe that lay on the floor among the frozen and soaked clothes in the utility room of the Thompsons' Sand Point cottage.

Moments earlier, while he called 9-1-1 seeking help, Nick had watched the pipe fall out of the Ice Man's belt. The stranger, wild-eyed and trembling, had only mumbled incoherently as Gary and his sons peeled away the cold, wet layers of clothing. Then Nora and her daughters had walked him in his long johns into the living room, where new logs had been added to the fireplace.

The weight of the pipe surprised Nick. He peered into one end—concrete. He flipped it around and examined the other end, which had a galvanized cap that made it look like a pipe bomb. He figured it must weigh four or five pounds, and wondered why an angler would carry such a tool.

Nick placed the pipe on a bench and then picked up the stranger's parka and snowmobile suit. They, too, were heavy, soaked with ice and water. He placed them in the washtub in the entryway. A large pool of water had formed on the linoleum floor, so he used a mop to wick up the water.

As he joined the others in the living room, Nick could not shake the image of the pipe from his mind. It lingered as he mulled what connection it might have to ice fishing.

The Ice Man, still in his wet thermal underwear, sat on a wooden chair in front of the fireplace, draped in two blue-and-white wool blankets. Full-size beach towels wrapped his feet. Another large towel collected the water dripping from the seat of the chair.

"Gotta go get my dad," the stranger said, his breathing labored, like his body was still trying to shake the cold. "He's out in the lake.

Gotta get him out."

"Help is on the way," Nora said, trying to comfort the distraught and confused young man. "Where is your dad? Where did you come from?" She rubbed the stranger's shoulders and upper arms to enhance his circulation and help warm him.

The Ice Man shook and continued muttering about the ice and snow. Between garbled words and ramblings, his teeth chattered like a Veg-O-Matic mincing celery. His lips had the hue of blueberries, and his eyes were glossy. His knees bounced up and down—anything to get warm. Gary piled more wood in the fireplace.

Nora placed another blanket around the stranger, then turned to her husband. "Should we go out and see if the dad is out there wandering around or lying in the snow?"

"I turned the floodlights on," Gary said, moving toward the front picture window. Except for the glow from the big lights, the lake was pitch black. "I could see our friend here's tracks in the snow, leading down to the lake. Nothing out there to the edge of the light, but we'll get some flashlights and rope from the shed and take a look."

The Thompson men dressed for the cold and hurried outside. Nora and her daughters tried to comfort the shivering stranger, who had not been able to reveal in any detail what had happened.

Nick went into the kitchen and used his cell phone to call Drayton Clapper. A dramatic story, no matter how it turned out, was unfolding in front of him, and he thought he should alert his boss.

The cell rang a half-dozen times. Then Nick heard the familiar gravelly voice: "Clapper, what's up?"

"Drayton, this is Steele. Wanted to give you a heads-up about what's happening out here on Sand Point. Got a pretty wild story in the works."

"Give it to me quick."

"Looks like one ice fisherman went into the lake but made it to shore. Says his dad is still missing," Nick said, trying to keep his voice low. "Dark and cold out there. Rescue unit on the way."

"What happened?" Clapper asked urgently, like his news radar had suddenly kicked into gear. "What's the guy who made it saying?"

"Not making much sense—may be in shock," Nick said. "He's just rambling on about helping his dad."

"Sounds good, Nick. First deadline is nine, which means you've got about two hours to file a story. Steve is on tonight—I'll have him save you a hole. But once I do, you've got to fill it."

Nick clicked off his cell and returned to the living room. Someone had put on soft Christmas music and a fresh pot of coffee. Nora was now sitting in a chair next to the Ice Man, her right arm around the young guy. He had finally stopped muttering, but his chin rested on his chest. Between sobs, he talked to the nurse, who offered him comfort and hope.

"You're okay now, Tom," she said over and over, gently rocking the young man. "My guys are outside looking for your dad, and more help is on the way."

What a big heart she had, Nick thought. He admired how Nora had taken in the Ice Man, now identified as Tom, and offered him warmth, and a shoulder on which to cry.

"It's not a good idea to go back outside right now, Tom," Nora was saying, her voice barely above a whisper. "You need to warm up and rest. You've been through an incredible ordeal."

The reporter looked through the front door at the lake to see if he could locate Gary and his sons. Moonlight reflected off the fresh snow covering the ice, illuminating the lake. Nick spotted them about a hundred yards out. For a moment he wondered if they had gone out too far, given the shaky condition of the ice. He had the urge to step out on the front deck and yell for the men to return.

Outside in the distance, Nick heard a siren. In minutes, the ambulance would pull into the driveway of the cottage.

He looked back out at the lake. The rope Gary had taken from the garage linked the three men about twenty-five feet apart. Suddenly they stopped moving and then turned back toward shore. The reporter watched them walking, spread apart but still linked by the rope, until he felt confident that they were okay.

Red and white lights danced across the walls of the kitchen and dining area as the ambulance halted in the cottage driveway. Two EMS personnel, carrying small black bags, rushed to the back door. One of the Thompson daughters directed them to the living room, where by now the Ice Man had somewhat thawed.

Nora identified herself as an RN and gave the paramedics vital background information as they poked and prodded the victim. While they worked on the young man, another set of flashing lights pulled in front of the cottage—that turned out to be the chief of the Fairview Township Fire Department, who also headed the community's water rescue teams in both winter and summer.

At nearly the same time, Nick saw Gary and his sons stepping up onto the shore. He grabbed his coat and hat and hurried out the back door, hailing Gary and directing him to the chief. The chief knew Nick from previous stories the reporter had developed.

Introductions by Nick were brief. Gary told the chief that he and his sons had followed the stranger's tracks out onto the lake. They had taken turns yelling for the missing man but had received no response.

How far they'd walked and what they had seen were the chief's first questions. Gary said they'd gone only as far as he felt comfortable; when they reached the point where he estimated the water was about chest deep, he had told his boys to stop. But they had seen nothing ahead, other than the tracks they were following.

The chief, a short, burly middle-aged man with a walrus mustache, said he had rescue units—an ice boat and cold-water div-ers—on the way, but he wasn't sure how much they would be able to do in the dark. "We want to find the missing man as fast as we can, but I got to protect my guys too," he said.

The chief told them the Coast Guard was currently responding to emergencies on the Lake St. Clair and Lake Huron coastlines. They had been alerted to the emergency on Sand Point too, but he didn't have many details to share.

The men were interrupted by the paramedics wheeling the Ice Man through the cottage back door and onto the deck. The sound of the stretcher rolling across wooden planks drowned out any chance for more communication. The men watched the victim, who stared straight up into the night as he was pushed down the driveway toward the ambulance's open back door.

"Better go see if I can talk with him now," the chief said, turning away from Nick and the Thompson men. "Thanks, guys. Stay off the ice, okay? Don't need to be fishing anybody else out right now."

The chief, with Nick on his heels, caught up with the rolling gurney as it reached the back of the EMS wagon. The chief asked the older paramedic if he could get a few minutes to talk with the victim.

"Hey, it sounds like we've got a missing man out here," the chief said. "Every minute counts. Anything I can get from him right now is critical."

The rescuer nodded but said the victim needed to be hospitalized right away. "He's suffering from hypothermia and rambling. Talk to the RN inside. She's bound to know more than anybody else here. She worked with him real well. May have saved his life."

Without slowing, the paramedics loaded the Ice Man into the ambulance and whisked him away.

Nick and the chief watched the EMS rig pull out, siren blaring and lights flashing. Nothing was said until the chief turned to head back to the cottage.

"Nick, I can't stop you from writing about what you're seeing here," he said, his head down, leaning into the wind and the light snow that pecked at their bare skin like tiny needles. The two men marched ahead, almost reaching a jog to get back inside. "Obviously you were invited here by the property owners, and that's okay. But do not quote me in your story in any way without clearing it with me. This is a very touchy situation, and I don't want to be misquoted in the paper. Do you understand me—completely?"

"Got it, chief," Nick said, hustling to keep up as they reached the cottage. "I'm definitely going to put a story together for tomorrow's paper—I just don't know what it is yet. But I will make sure that you're okay with anything I attribute to you."

Nick checked his watch. It was nearly eight o'clock, just an hour before the first deadline, and the reporter had not written a word yet. But there were still lots of missing pieces to this puzzle.

The men reached the back deck, where they could see the Thompson family just inside the cottage. Gary and the boys were pulling off their winter gear while Nora comforted her daughters, who were no doubt shaken by what they had observed and experienced: one man in danger after a harrowing experience on the ice, and another missing, condition unknown. The evening's disturbing events would cause most folks to lose their composure. Sleep in this household would only come from exhaustion.

Whirling red, white, and blue lights flashed across the back of the cottage, capturing the attention of the chief and the reporter. It was a sheriff's department cruiser.

The chief groaned. "And things were going so well. Let's keep going and talk to the Thompsons. The deputy will catch up soon enough."

When they got inside, Nora told them she had little to report. "Most of what he said was incoherent—rambling. He kept repeating himself," she said. "I'm afraid hypothermia was playing with his mind. Kind of delirious. He got better as he warmed up some."

The chief nodded, and Nick scribbled notes as Nora briefed them on what else the Ice Man had told her as the two sat in front of the fireplace. The nurse was holding up well from the stress of the evening, but the reporter did notice a slight tremor in her right hand.

A knock at the door interrupted them. Nora opened the door for Deputy Jay-Bob Ratchett.

"Well, what in the gol-durned heck is going on?" Jay-Bob asked, stepping into the entryway and sliding up to the group. He gave the Thompsons a quick look-see, then focused his attention on the guy with the notebook. Nick introduced himself and stuck his right hand out to shake. The deputy grabbed his mitt and held it so no more notes could be written.

"How in the gol-durned heck did you get here from Bay City before I got here from over by the state park?" he asked, not letting go of Nick's hand. "Now, you know you can't write nothin' until we send out a press release in the morning, right?"

"No, deputy. I've been here since late this afternoon," Nick said. "In about an hour I will be filing a story about what I've witnessed and learned here."

"Wonderful—would somebody please fill me in?" Jay-Bob said. "From what I heard on the radio, we've still got a man missing. And one guy on the way to the hospital? I passed the ambulance on the way here. I've got to file a report."

The chief and Nora updated the deputy. Nick wandered off toward the fireplace to write his story.

Chapter 12

Nick opened his apartment door and reached down for his copy of *The Bay City Blade*. The Sunday advertising insert—about twenty slick pages—spilled out onto the floor of the entryway just as Jenni, the landlord's big, slobbering chocolate Lab, came bounding up the stairwell. She jumped up as Nick gathered the ads. The dog's long, wet tongue jabbed at Nick's face while she steadied herself with a paw on his shoulder.

The reporter opened his door and brought the paper and the dog inside. Jenni found her bowl with a treat already in it, and Nick reintroduced himself to the fat, fluffy rocker in his living room to drink coffee and read. He opened up the paper and was delighted to see his story on the front page.

Ice angler missing, son recovering from hypothermia
By Nick Steele

A Huron County farmer and his son broke through the ice while fishing late Saturday afternoon on Wild Fowl Bay near Sand Point. The father was still missing this morning, and the son was in serious but stable condition at Scheurer Hospital in Pigeon.

The anglers, identified by witnesses as Carl Huffmann and his son, Thomas, were riding 4-wheelers and towing a sled with their fishing gear when they went into the icy water. Witnesses said the son was able to walk to shore in the dark after going into the water as evening approached. It is unclear how far out on the bay the anglers were when the ice broke, but authorities believe the survivor walked for 45 minutes, possibly more.

Nora Thompson, a registered nurse who owns a cottage on the south shore of Sand Point, said she and her husband, Gary, heard a knock at their lakeside door just after 6 p.m.

"We opened the door and found a young man covered in ice and snow," she said. "I was shocked. He was muttering about needing to get help for his dad. We got him in, tried to warm him up and called 9-1-1."

Later, Thompson said, the young man told her he thought he had wandered on the ice for about an hour, but he was not sure of the length of time. She said the younger Huffmann had walked toward the most visible lights on the south shore, the family's exterior Christmas tree lights, strung on a tall pine.

Rescue teams followed the son's tracks in the snow out onto Wild Fowl Bay. At press time, midnight, Carl Huffmann had not been found.

"We had divers and an ice boat out looking, but searching in the dark on mushy ice is very difficult," said Ben Canfield, the Fairview Township fire chief, who also oversees emergency rescue crews. "We've put a call in for the Coast Guard to send a chopper. We're doing everything we can to locate Mr. Huffmann."

Tom Huffmann told the Thompsons that he and his dad were able to pull themselves out of the water after they initially broke through. But he said the men broke through the ice a second time. Though the younger man said they got themselves back out, he had lost track of his dad while they walked toward shore.

Huron County Sheriff's Deputy J.R. Ratchett said the Huffmanns run a large farming operation in the southern part of Huron County, near the Tuscola County line. Ratchett said family members were notified Saturday night.

When contacted by The Blade, Betty Huffmann said she was on

her way to visit her stepson, Tom, in the hospital. She asked for prayers for her missing husband.

"Carl has been ice fishing out there for the last 40 years," she said. "He's experienced. He knows what he's doing. All we can do is pray."

The incident on Wild Fowl Bay was one of six emergency calls the sheriff's department received from ice anglers on Saturday. None of the other calls resulted in serious injury.

Ratchett and Canfield said searches would intensify this morning for Carl Huffmann.

Nick dropped the paper in his lap. He had already spoken with his boss, and he would be heading back to Sand Point right after breakfast. The reporter wanted to stay on top of the search for Carl Huffmann, but he also wanted to talk with the survivor if Tom had recovered enough from the ordeal. He wanted all the details of what had happened out on the ice.

As Nick stroked the top of Jenni's head and thumbed through the newspaper, a news bulletin came over the radio. WSGW's Bill Hewitt, the area's top news broadcaster when it came to covering fires, robberies, murders, and car crashes in the Tri-Cities, reported that divers had recovered Mr. Huffmann's body from Wild Fowl Bay.

Nick leaned over and turned up the volume for Hewitt's report. The body, he learned, was found under a ledge of ice about two hundred yards from where two 4-wheelers bobbed upside down in the water. Rescuers had brought Mr. Huffmann to shore and attempted to resuscitate the man using cold-water rescue techniques. The victim was declared dead at the scene, Hewitt said. The younger Huffmann was still listed in serious but stable condition at Scheurer

Hospital.

Nick flicked off the radio and folded his newspaper just as his cell phone rang. Caller ID told him it was his longtime friend and fellow reporter Dave Balz.

"So what time are we going out to the Thumb?" Dave said. "Saw your piece this morning—figured you'd already be working on a follow-up."

Nick said he would be leaving within the hour. "I'll swing by and bring the coffee. You supply the donuts."

Nick took Jenni back down to Mrs. Babcock's first-floor apartment. The reporter adored his landlord, who was shorter and thinner than a jockey but just as no-nonsense and feisty as a rider nearing the finish line with a whip. He tried the doorknob to her place. It turned freely. He let Jenni in the door, gave her a quick pat on the head, and pulled it shut.

As he headed back upstairs to finish getting ready, Nick heard his landlord's high-pitched voice through the closed door: "Thanks for bringing Jenni back, Nick. Have a good day and dress warm. It will be cold out on the Thumb near the lake."

Nick smiled, thinking that Mrs. Babcock knew him too well. He grabbed his gear, poured a thermos of steaming black coffee, and made his way out to the apartment parking lot. His gold Firebird sat in a corner spot under the carport, hogging two spaces.

The 'Bird's big V-8 rumbled to life, and Nick aimed his baby in the direction of Dave's place. The news of Mr. Huffmann's death saddened him. When Nick left Sand Point Saturday night, he'd been hopeful that Tom Huffmann's dad would be discovered. But he'd also known the prospects of him being found alive became slimmer with each passing hour.

The reporter's goals had changed. Today he would gather background information on the elder Huffmann so that he could write a worthy obituary for the longtime Thumb farmer. He would also pull together the latest search and rescue information to spice up the obituary with news from the accident. Certainly, new details would emerge now that a death had been confirmed and the survivor had had a full night of recovery in hospital care.

Dave was dressed like an Eskimo when Nick pulled up at his place. He wore a winter parka with a hood and fake fur around the exterior edge. Leather mittens, a pair of Carhartt bib overalls, and snowmobile boots completed his preparation for venturing into the cold. Under one arm Dave carried a box of Krispy Kreme donuts.

"Ah, my arteries are aching just looking at those yummies," Nick said. "But you are forgiven. Hop in. We'll be on Sand Point in about an hour."

Nick had already called the Thompsons, who'd okayed him to drop by their place that morning. No one at the house had gotten much sleep with rescue vehicles and searchlights scanning the area most of the night.

The drive northeast from Bay City on M-25 was easy traveling. Despite the snow flurries late Saturday afternoon, the state highway was clear and dry. Sunday morning traffic was light. Occasionally the sun poked through the overcast sky, making Nick shield his eyes from the warm rays.

Nick sipped coffee and chewed on gooey pastry while he updated Dave with the background information he hadn't revealed in his page-one story. His friend was fascinated by how the news had unfolded right in front of Nick while he was working on an unrelated story.

Nick also told Dave about the piece of pipe he'd found among the survivor's wet clothing at the cottage. "I don't know what to make of the pipe," he said. "Why would you have something that looks and feels like a weapon out on an ice-fishing adventure?"

"Dunno," Dave said, picking apart a donut. "Maybe he had it with him in case they hauled in a monster catfish or pike and had to conk it out. That'd be a good question for somebody who practices the sport, which ain't me."

After a moment of silence, Nick asked Dave what he'd missed at O'Hare's Pub on Saturday night. It had been another wild night of revelry at the Bay City West Side bar, Dave said. He described how a woman, obviously too tipsy to feel pain, had stood on a table and tried to pull down Nick's pants, which had been stapled to the ceiling of the pub for three years—the result of a lost wager. It was a noble effort, but she had failed miserably and was escorted from the bar with bruised feelings and a shiner from hitting a coat rack when she fell.

The two friends laughed. As they neared their destination, Nick asked if he'd missed anything worthwhile in the *Blade* newsroom. "Same BS, different day," Dave said.

When the reporters pulled into the Thompsons' driveway on Sand Point, Nice Nurse Nora had just returned from visiting the Ice Man at Scheurer Hospital. Nick introduced his friend and Nora invited them into the cottage, cautioning them that the family might still be asleep.

"Gary was up most of the night and into this morning, watching the rescue teams out on the ice," she said, fatigue showing on her face. Her eyes were red and puffy. "It was very emotional when they brought Mr. Huffmann's body to shore. So very, very sad."

Nick asked about the condition of the survivor.

"He's doing pretty good," she said, pouring three cups of coffee. Nick studied the woman. She looked older, the lines in her face deeper. Though the tremor in her right hand was not visible, she seemed distracted, perhaps even overwhelmed by all that had happened in the past eighteen hours. She had forgotten to remove her Spartan green knit cap and scarf.

"Are you okay?" Nick asked, leaning toward her to offer comfort. "You look exhausted. What can I do for you?"

Nora waved off the offer. "Nothing some sleep won't cure. I just can't get over what happened," she said, joining the men at the table. She fidgeted with the spoon at the side of her cup. "I've been a nurse for a lot of years, and I've seen just about every kind of accident and injury you can imagine, but what happened last night really hit me.

"We had one man die out there on the ice and a second man narrowly escape death. If he had fallen into the water a third time or become disoriented from hypothermia while he was still walking, that kid would have been a goner too. Don't know if he realizes that yet."

The nurse sipped her coffee. Steam rose from the cup. The cottage was silent except for Gary's distant snoring and the occasional snorts for air coming from one of the back bedrooms. Nick jotted some notes in his reporter's pad, letting Nora's thoughts settle for a few minutes.

Finally Dave asked if the survivor had suffered frostbite. Nora said his fingertips showed signs of frostnip and superficial frostbite, the earliest stages. The nurse said the young man had lost his gloves and knit cap when he went into the water, but he was smart enough to cup his fingers and stick them into his parka pockets much of the time he was wandering on the ice.

Nick was curious whether she had run into any Huffmann family members when she visited the Ice Man. The reporter was hoping he could meet with them while he and Dave were in the Thumb.

"Only visitor I saw was a girlfriend, who was there with her sister," Nora said. "I didn't stay long—just wanted to check on him.

Offer some comfort."

"I'll bet he appreciated that." Nick took a swig of his coffee. "Kind of strange, though, that nobody from the family was at the hospital. Or am I reading that wrong?"

"I think everyone is in various states of shock, so sometimes that can seem kind of strange," Nora said. She put her cup down and walked from the table to the counter, loading the toaster with half bagels. She pulled homemade jam from the refrigerator and placed it on the table in front of the reporters. Nick thought he noticed Dave starting to drool, and elbowed him, motioning for him to mop his lower lip.

"Tom cried when I hugged him," Nora said. "We're going to stay in touch. I feel very sorry for that young guy. He's in the same age range as my kids—it's going to be tough to sort it all out." She placed the toasted bagels on small plates on the table. Dave dug in, grunting his appreciation.

Nick asked if she thought the reporters could get in to see Tom at the hospital.

"You can try if you like, but you might have better luck talking with family members at the Huffmann house," Nora said, nodding to Dave, who had scarfed down the breakfast treat in three bites. "Hey there, big guy. Slow down a little. Don't bite your fingers off— there's more if you like."

"Man, you just had some donuts on the way here," Nick said, shaking his head in disbelief at his partner.

"Sorry." Dave looked from Nora to Nick. "Don't want to act swinish, but boy, is this stuff good. Thanks!"

Nick thanked Nora too and decided it was a good time for the two to leave; the nurse had been very hospitable, but she clearly needed rest. And, Nick thought, Dave needed to quit eating.

Nora, ever gracious, told Nick he could call her anytime he liked.

She said she was going to clean up the kitchen, then find a quiet place to sleep. Later they could finish the interview they had started when the Ice Man banged on her front door.

Nick thought of one last question as they walked toward the back entryway of the house. "When I was cleaning up the melted mess on the floor here last night, I found a piece of pipe," he said. "It was tangled up in the gear Tom was wearing when he came into the cottage. Never seen anything quite like it, but I'm not a fisherman. Is that some kind of tool or device that somebody ice fishing would use?"

Gary had spotted it too, Nora said. She pointed to the garage with her chin. "It's out there with the rest of Tom's stuff. Gary wondered if it had something to do with one of the 4-wheelers the guys were riding."

"I was going to ask about it last night, but everybody kinda had their hands full," Nick said. "I got a couple of buddies who ice fish. I'll run it by them—see what they think."

The reporters said good-bye and drove down Sand Point, passing tall pines covered with light snow. Giant oaks dotted each side of Crescent Beach Road. They were headed for Pigeon, a small farming community seven miles south of Sand Point.

"What a sweet woman," Dave said as they drove. "And a beautiful place on the lake. I don't believe I've ever seen such a fabulous setting—it's like something you'd see on a postcard."

As they neared Pigeon, Scheurer Hospital, a sprawling campus on both sides of Caseville Road, came into view. Scheurer, employing hundreds of mostly local folks and caring for thousands throughout the area, had become one of the essential sources of employment and economic vitality in the community. The hospital also had a helicopter landing pad for patients who had to be transported to the big cities in central or southern Michigan for more specialized care.

When Nick stopped at the front desk, he learned that only family members were allowed visitation. He did, however, discover that Tom Huffmann's condition had been upgraded to stable, which probably meant he would be discharged fairly soon.

Nick asked the front desk clerk, a young woman whom the reporter pegged at about twenty, if she happened to know Tom Huffmann. She said she remembered him from high school, but he was older—they weren't friends and didn't socialize. He asked the clerk if any family members were currently in the waiting area. The clerk did not say anything but shook her head.

Nick thought it odd that Tom Huffmann had no visitors waiting to see him as he recovered. Dave said he didn't find it that unusual, given that the cold, stiff body of the family patriarch had just been discovered hours earlier.

"I suppose," Nick said, though he still had a funny feeling about it. The reporter decided to head for the Huffmann homestead, a massive spread hugging the southern boundary of Huron County west and south of Owendale, a tiny country town that over the years had shrunk to a bar, a convenience store, a grain elevator, and a small school district as the area's farming operations grew in size. He had gotten the address from the telephone book at the Thompsons'.

"But are we being insensitive?" he said as he pointed the Firebird in the direction of the Huffmanns'. "Is the family going to look at us as a couple of coldhearted bloodsuckers just out to get a story?"

"Maybe," Dave said. "But who gives a shit, really? We've got a job to do. Worst-case scenario: We bang on the door, identify ourselves, and humbly ask to speak with Mrs. Huffmann. They say no, and we head home."

"Right," Nick said. "Best case scenario: They say, 'Come right in,' and then we've got a really good piece for Monday's paper no matter what we discover. Makes sense to me. Let's go for it."

"Plus," Dave said, "they might feed us again too."

Nick rolled his eyes. He was amazed at his friend's massive appetite for food and for life, but he was glad to have a partner with such good news instincts.

The two drove on, passing one farm field after another until the cropland seemed to run together, stretching in every possible direction. Occasionally farmhouses and barns or storage sheds would appear.

"How will we know when we reach the Huffmann property?" Dave asked. "The land is indistinguishable—we may be driving by part of their place right now."

Nick looked off in the distance as a massive white house came into view, sitting up on a hill an eighth of a mile or so back from the main road. A huge covered wraparound porch graced the two-story home, and windows with forest-green shutters lined each floor. A detached four-car garage and two other giant storage buildings stood in the background.

An arch with a sign spanned the entrance to the driveway: "Huffmann Acres." In smaller lettering underneath, it read: "Feeding American families near and far for more than 100 years." A five-foot fieldstone fence ran in each direction from the arch. Three staggered rows of white pines stood behind the stone fencing.

Nick let the 'Bird idle as he and Dave soaked in the grandeur. A half-dozen cars and a handful of pickup trucks filled the driveway near the house. Interior lights illuminated what looked like the front living room, behind a massive picture window.

The reporter gunned the engine twice, then slowly let out the clutch, easing the vehicle into the driveway. "Let's go bang on the door and give it a shot," Nick said. Dave did not respond, nodding silently.

Rather than trying the front door, they decided to use the side door nearest the garage. Nick guessed it might be the kitchen or a back utility room. Light shone brightly through the windows, and he could hear people talking. He rapped on the door with his knuckles.

An older woman, thick in the neck, with tired eyes and her hands hardened by farm work, greeted the men. She was dressed in black from head to toe.

"Hello, I'm looking for Mrs. Huffmann," Nick said. "I know the timing is probably not good right now, but I was wondering if I could speak with her?" He held the door open with his left hand. It was a utility room, but it led directly to a large country kitchen that was filled with people talking in low tones.

The woman asked Nick and Dave to wait at the door while she looked for Mrs. Huffmann. But Nick did not let the door close. In the kitchen the chatter continued; Nick could see the visitors and figured they were neighbors who had come to pay their respects to the family.

"Yes, what can I do for you?" Betty Huffmann said, smiling uneasily as she approached with her hands on her hips. She was wearing a blue floral dress with a high collar. Its hem hung beneath her knees. She was tall and slender, with hair as dark as the circles around her eyes.

Nick introduced himself and his sidekick. "I hate to intrude like this, but we're from *The Bay City Blade*. We were wondering if you'd talk with us for a few minutes about the terrible tragedy your family experienced last night and this morning."

Betty nodded and directed the reporters to follow the porch around to the front of the house. Friends and neighbors were visiting with family in the kitchen, she said. But she told the reporters she would be happy to meet with them in the front sitting room instead.

As the reporters moved toward the front door, Dave spoke in a low voice. "Boy, did we get lucky. Awful nice of her to talk with us. Could have just kicked us to the curb."

"You bet, except there are no curbs out here," Nick said, walking ahead of his friend. "We may only get a few minutes with her, so I'm going to ask about the husband first, then the son."

Dave nodded. "This will be touchy." He said he would take notes and observe.

The new widow held the front door open for the reporters, and they entered the foyer. A glass chandelier dangled from the high point of the vaulted ceiling. Closets with hinged six-panel oak doors lined one side of the foyer, and a sitting bench ran along the opposite side. The reporters took off their wet boots. Without saying anything, they surveyed the entrance and front room, surprised at the magnificence of the farmhouse.

Nick could hear laughter coming from the kitchen. Rock music blared from behind a closed door down the hall from the front room, which was big enough to comfortably seat a marching band. A fieldstone fireplace covered the main interior wall of the room. But exterior windows stretching from near the ceiling to just above the floor allowed natural light to flood the massive room and give it a warm, open feel.

Mrs. Huffmann sat on a long dark-brown leather couch. A wooden coffee table with a marble top separated her and the matching couch, where the reporters took a seat. The woman of the household offered to get them coffee and a slice of the cake that one of the neighbors had brought that morning.

"Thanks, that's very kind," Nick said. "But we do not want to impose any more than we have. Appreciate you meeting with us. We'll make this quick so you can return to your guests."

The smell of warm baked goods wafted through the home.

Dave's bird-dog nose for home cooking went on high alert, but he fought mightily to stay focused on the job at hand. He pulled out his notebook and waited for Nick.

Nick started by asking what time her husband had been found and what information the rescuers had shared with her. Had they given her any details about her husband's recovery? he said.

"They found Carl about eight this morning, right after first light," she said, looking down at her hands while she twisted a small white handkerchief. "They had been searching in teams all night with no luck. Coast Guard helicopter, portable floodlights, everything. He'd been in the lake all night."

"Was he close to where the two of them broke through?" Nick asked, turning a page in his notebook.

"No, he was several hundred yards away from where they found the 4-wheelers," she said, sitting up straight and facing the reporters. "He was under about ten inches of ice. They said one of the rescuers spotted the bright-blue scarf that I had gotten him for Christmas last year. Otherwise his body would have just been another shadow under the ice." Betty stood and walked to the giant picture window, peering out across the frozen farm fields. She kneaded the hanky in her hands. After a few moments she returned to talk with the reporters again.

Nick asked if rescuers had found anything unusual when the body was recovered.

"Carl had a gash on his forehead, about four inches long, just over his right eye," Betty said, making direct eye contact with Nick. "One of the guys said it looked like he might have hit his head on the 4-wheeler when he was in the water. A bang on the head, hypothermia, the shock of hitting ice-cold water—all of that might have caused confusion." She stood again, and this time she paced back and forth in front of the reporters as she spoke. "Lord knows what was going through his mind at the time. He probably was not thinking clearly, or he might have saved himself. Carl was a very tough, strong man.

"Plus, he had lost his parka—no gloves or hat either," she said. "Glad he had that scarf on, though, or they probably would still be out there looking for him."

Mention of a gash on Carl's head reminded Nick about the chunk of pipe in Tom's cold-weather gear. He looked at Dave, who had underlined and circled "4-inch gash over right" in his notebook.

"What about your son?" Nick asked, turning another page. He studied the woman closely. "How's he doing this morning?"

"My stepson is doing okay," she said. "I haven't been to the hospital yet today, but they say he should be discharged in the morning."

Nick mentioned that he had been visiting the cottage on Sand Point when Tom showed up at the door after walking off the lake. The young man was lucky, the reporter said, to have found help when he did.

"Yup, you're right. Lucky," Betty said, letting the word linger. "Just too bad he wasn't able to help his dad."

"Did you talk to Tom last night?" Nick asked.

"We saw him at the hospital, but he was mumbling and talking in riddles." She took her seat again and patted her upper lip with the handkerchief, then folded the cloth in her lap. "Just kept going on and on about losing track of Carl. Walking out on the ice, falling into old fishing holes. Said he didn't know how he made it."

The rock music intensified, and Nick looked up to see a young woman emerge into the hallway. She scampered into the kitchen, where more voices could be heard.

"That's my daughter, Katie," Betty said. "She's got some friends over to help her pass the time. Kids. Never know what they're thinking."

"Is she Carl's daughter too?" Nick asked, watching the door that led to the kitchen. The reporter heard voices in the kitchen offering the young woman condolences and support. She responded with curt thanks and nervous giggles.

"Nope, she's mine. Tom is Carl's youngest."

Betty's comment about the kids made her choke up with emotion. Tears welled in her eyes and spilled down her cheeks in droplets the size of peas. She lifted the hanky to dab and catch them just as Dave offered a handkerchief from his hip pocket. It was matted stiff, stuck together at two of the corners. Betty looked at the soiled rag, horrified enough to stop the tears. "Thanks, but I'm okay." She twirled her hanky in her hands again, her gaze averted to the floor.

After a few minutes of silence, Katie backed through the door, carrying a two-liter bottle of pop, a plate of cookies, and a bag of potato chips. The blond young woman waved and smiled at the reporters and her mother.

But when she saw her mom's distress, she placed the treats on a table and went to her side. "I'm so sorry, Mommy. I know we're all hurting." Katie knelt on the floor and pulled her mom close. "Time will help us heal," she said in a voice so soft that the reporters could barely hear her.

Both women wept quietly.

Nick took a deep breath and waited in silence. Dave pulled his stained handkerchief apart and blew his nose into it, startling the women and prompting a glare from Nick. Dave stuffed the filthy cloth back in his jeans.

Finally Betty thanked Katie and suggested she tend to her friends. The young woman picked up her snacks and scooted back into the room where Kurt Cobain bellowed about the ills of the world. The door slammed shut behind her, muffling the noise disguised as music.

Katie's brief appearance had thrown the interview off track. Nick waited a moment in silence. He jotted fresh notes, allowing Betty to refocus. Then he asked if Carl and Tom were experienced ice anglers.

"Heck yes," Betty said, regaining her composure after the tender moment with her daughter. "They had been out on Saginaw Bay hundreds of times over the years, whether together or with friends. They crashed through the ice before too—several times, in fact. But they always fished in shallow water, usually the canals on Sand Point."

Betty was up again, pacing and twisting the hanky again. She stared at the floor as she talked to the reporters. "This time, for some reason, they were way out on the bay in deeper water and further from shore. Don't know what they were thinking. Tom can probably tell you when he's back on his feet."

The kitchen door swung open again, and a neighbor told Betty that she and her husband were getting ready to leave. The woman looked distraught. Her eyes were swollen and her nose was red. Her voice cracked slightly as she spoke to Mrs. Huffmann.

Betty excused herself to walk her friends out. Nick and Dave stood too, using the interruption as their cue to make a timely exit. Nick asked Betty if he could call her at another, less hectic time. He said he was sure he would have more questions.

"Call anytime," Betty told them, adding that she would put together a full obituary later in the afternoon. She promised to ask the Owendale funeral home to email it to them.

The reporters thanked the woman for meeting with them at such a difficult time. Nick and Dave left through the same door they'd entered. Other visitors were in the driveway, some coming and some going.

Snow flurries, the kind made up of big, fluffy flakes, fluttered in the cold air. Heavy cloud cover blocked rays of sunshine from changing the mood of this dark and dreary day.

When they got back out on the road, they watched the farm-house become smaller and smaller as they crawled away from the Huffmann spread. It gave them time to absorb what they'd just experienced. Very unusual for reporters to get so close to a family so soon after tragedy.

Dave was the first to speak. "Whoa, very dramatic. We're lucky the family would actually talk to us some. Looks like a lot of pain going on."

Nick agreed, but he decided to tell Dave about the cement-filled pipe. It had been nagging at him since he first saw it in the Thompson home. Betty's revelation that Carl had a head injury suddenly gave the pipe new relevance.

"I've got to step forward with what I know about the pipe," he said. "It could be evidence."

Dave nodded. "Why else would he be carrying it on a fishing trip?"

That question prompted many more. Nick wondered aloud about Mrs. Huffmann, who he knew had been married before. "Is she from the Thumb? Where did she and Katie come from? How did they end up in Carl's life and home?" He used Dave as a sounding board, bouncing ideas off him as they drove. Nick knew the questions would spark Dave's growing interest in the story.

Dave volunteered to check into Betty's background. He said he would snoop around the Pigeon and Owendale communities first, to see what was known about her and her daughter. "I'll start by having a cold one at the Pigeon Inn," Dave said. "Maybe buy a round or two, see if I can get anyone to casually talk about the family and its horrible tragedy." He shifted his large frame in the bucket seat to face Nick. A smile spread across his face. "If that doesn't work, I'll try the local beauty salon."

"Yeah, good idea," Nick said. "You look like you're due for a cut anyway—maybe get your roots done and add some highlights. I'm sure you'll fit right in."

Dave grinned at his friend. "And if there's a bunch of ladies in that salon, I'll come away with a cut, some good info, and a phone number or two."

"You sound pretty sure of yourself," Nick said with a laugh. He shifted gears, heading back toward Bay City.

"I got my ways, and you got yours."

Chapter 13

Deputy Jay-Bob Ratchett walked slowly down a long hallway in Scheurer Hospital. His head swiveled from left to right and back again as he slowed to peek into patient rooms. He nodded and smiled at nurses and orderlies. Every few doors, he recognized a patient or a visitor and shouted out a greeting.

"Hey, Bob, you ol' three-legged coyote, what you doin' back in here again," he said, pulling up at a room where three visitors stood around a bed containing one of the deputy's old schoolmates.

"It's my back. Just can't seem to get it straightened out," Bob replied. He fidgeted in his bed. "You visiting or working today?"

"Little of both," Jay-Bob said, leaning on the doorframe with one arm. "Saying hey and baling some hay while I'm here."

"Thanks for stopping, Boog! Good seeing ya!"

The deputy kept moving down the spotless corridor, which had a faint odor of chlorine, until he reached a room near the end of the hall. The door was closed. He paused to check the room number against the slip of paper he was carrying, then turned the knob.

Tom Huffmann lay in bed with a pillow over his face. He did not move or respond when the deputy said hello and asked quietly if he was awake. The room was empty except for the hospital bed, a tray on wheels, monitors, and a visitor's chair. Sunlight poured in through a large window with open blinds, giving the room a toasty feel.

Jay-Bob decided to take a seat and wait. After a moment he tried again. "Tom, I realize you might not feel like it, but we need to have a discussion. Won't take long, but I need to get some answers from you. Figurin' to stay here until we talk."

The pillow moved, but only slightly to one side—not enough for the deputy to see Tom's face. Then the young man rolled his body away from Jay-Bob without saying a word. The IV stand rattled, causing the bag of fluid and its tube to sway.

Silence. The deputy waited a few more moments, then said, "Need to know what happened out there. Your dad is dead, and you very nearly lost your life."

"I ... want ... to ... die," Tom said in a low whine. He still faced away from the deputy. "Couldn't save my old man. I should have died out there too. That's it—all I got to say."

"Well, that's not going to cut it. Roll over here so we can talk ... please," Jay-Bob said. "Once we're done, I'll leave you alone. A man died. The medical examiner has him now. I got a report to fill out."

Finally the young man complied, rolling back toward the deputy and swinging his legs down to the floor. The pillow fell from the bed. Tom sat up, grunted softly, and put his free hand to his face, massaging his temples and shielding himself from the deputy's gaze. He stared at the patterned ceramic tile.

Jay-Bob thanked him for cooperating. He pulled out a small notebook, informing the younger man that he had a recorder and was turning it on too—just procedure. He asked Tom to tell him what happened Saturday after he and his dad had pulled up at Mud Creek.

Tom cleared his throat and started his story, drawing it out a word at a time as if he was speaking solely for the recorder. He and his dad had unloaded their gear quickly, he said, hoping to make up for their late start. He recounted their run across the ice, the brief encounter with Jon Barrett, and the confrontation over their ice hole with the drunken angler. Tom talked about the fish they had caught and the conversation the two had shared. He told the deputy how they'd talked about his mom and some of the good times they'd had.

Jay-Bob asked if Tom and his dad had been on good terms lately. That question seemed to catch the young man off guard. The deputy watched Tom shift on the edge of his bed, looking down at the floor until he found his slippers. "No better or worse than usual, I guess. Why do you ask?"

"Word around town is that you and your dad had some serious differences of opinion," Jay-Bob said. "Just wondering how serious, and if you argued yesterday afternoon?"

"Yeah, it's no secret I hated my old man, and we scrapped from time to time," Tom said, leaning back to look out the window. Blackbirds chirped from the branches of a dormant tree in the snow-covered courtyard. He watched them take turns visiting a feeder to peck at cracked corn. "But when that ice collapses under you and you go ass over end into the freezing cold water, it changes," he said. "Everything is forgotten when you realize you're dancing with death. The past doesn't matter when you think you're goin' to die. It's all about survival."

The deputy jotted down notes, his tongue peeking out of the corner of his mouth as he worked his pen furiously. When he stopped, Jay-Bob paused to look back over what he had written. "How did you get out of the water?" he asked.

Tom shifted on the bed again, reaching for the Styrofoam cup of water on his tray. He shook the cup, rattling the ice, and the deputy looked up from his notebook.

"The water is a bitch when you can't touch the lake bottom," Tom said. "When you try to pull yourself up and out onto the ice, it just breaks away in big chunks. I almost got out a couple of times, but just couldn't quite make it.

"Same with the old man," he said, taking a sip from the cup and holding it up high enough to let a few half-melted ice cubes tumble into his mouth. "He probably outweighs me by a hundred pounds.

With gear and boots on, it feels like you're struggling with the weight of the world, and every minute you're getting colder."

Jay-Bob continued making notes, his tongue working as fast as his pen. He stopped every couple minutes to study the young man in front of him. As far as Jay-Bob was concerned, Tom Huffmann looked surprisingly good for a guy who, by fate or just pure shit luck, had escaped death by drowning or freezing less than twenty-four hours ago. But the deputy concluded that Tom's youth and good physical condition probably had more to do with his survival and quick recovery than anything else. "So how did you get out?" he asked.

"We kept breaking off chunks of ice and paddling toward shore," Tom said. He put his cup on the tray and swung his feet back up on the bed. Then he faced the deputy, leaning on one elbow. "When we came up on a sandbar where we could both touch bottom with our feet, the old man lifted me up and pushed me out. Luckily I landed on solid ice, so I stretched out as flat as I could and pulled him up too. Took some doin', but I got him out. We lay there a few minutes in that cold wind, absolutely freezing—too tired to move."

"Then what?" The deputy studied his face and body movements, hoping to read Tom beyond what his words revealed.

"We tried to get our bearings, but it was getting darker by the minute," Tom said. He flipped over in the bed to take the pressure off his shoulder, then lay on his back, staring at the ceiling as if he were looking for something. "The old man saw Christmas lights on the south shore of Sand Point, so we made that our landmark and started walking. But the ice broke up again around an old fishing hole, and the old man went all the way in.

"I went to help him, but this time he told me to keep going, keep heading for shore to get help. He was going back to the sandbar to get himself out, he said. Never saw him again." Tom covered his face with the pillow, which he'd retrieved from the floor. "I kept walking," he said, his voice muffled. "I fell into a fishing hole with one leg, then got out and walked some more. Took forever, but I finally got to shore and found the cottage with the lights."

The deputy could hear him weeping softly into the fluffy headrest. Tom's sobs were the only sounds in the room until a nurse walked in to check on her patient.

She touched the young man's arm and asked if he needed anything. "Can I get you some ice?"

"Wrong question," Jay-Bob said.

The nurse's eyes widened, and she covered her mouth with her free hand. "How about some cold water?"

The deputy could not suppress a grin. He shook his head at the nurse, who left the room, letting the door close behind her with a soft click.

Tom did not look up, saying no between sobs.

The young man's openness prompted Jay-Bob to bring up an important question. He decided to ask about the cut on Carl's forehead.

Tom sprang upright in his bed. "What cut?" He locked eyes with the deputy.

Jay-Bob moved forward in his chair, bringing the two men nearly face to face for the first time. "When they found your dad, the rescuers said he had a pretty sizable gash on his head. I'm sure it will be in the ME's report—he's not going to miss that. At what point did he get the cut? Did you see it happen?"

"I don't remember seeing any injuries to the old man's head, or any blood," Tom said, wiping his eyes with a corner of the bedsheet. He grabbed a handful of tissues from a box on the tray and blew his nose hard, disintegrating the see-through paper. "Must have hit his head after I saw him last."

The deputy scribbled a few more notes, then thanked Tom and asked when the young man would be released from the hospital. Tom said he hoped it would be the next morning; one of his older brothers was coming up from the city, and Tom would be staying with him for a while to sort things out.

"Sounds good," Jay-Bob said. The two shook hands, and Jay-Bob opened the door, saying he would be in touch if he needed more information.

As the deputy walked back to his cruiser, he couldn't get the discussion he'd just had with Tom Huffmann out of his mind. The young man's open assertion that he hated his dad and that he was aware it was well-known in the community ate at him.

That's because Deputy Ratchett was no stranger to such notions. Jay-Bob had grown up in the shadow of a man who was Mr. All-American Everything. Trent Ratchett had been the top athlete at Bad Axe High School, president of the student council, president of the senior class, and an honors student, and had dated the cheerleading captain (Jay-Bob's mom) and won the lead male role in the school play.

But a serious knee injury during Trent's freshman year of college had benched him permanently, ending all hope for collegiate sports. His life had gone into the crapper after that. Soon he'd dropped out of college and settled back in Bad Axe, ready to take a job selling insurance. When the cheer captain became pregnant, he'd decided to get married and focus on family. Little James Robert would be everything—and accomplish everything—that Trent could not.

As Jay-Bob drove toward the Huffmann farm, he recalled the many nights as a youngster when he went to bed cursing his father and wishing that a fatal car accident would relieve him and his mother of their pain. He could never fulfill his dad's dreams and had no desire to make him happy. Jay-Bob also remembered feeling ashamed of such thoughts but did not regret them. To this day, the father and son rarely spoke. They did not spend holidays together.

The deputy turned onto the road leading to the Huffmann farm and tried to ditch the horrible feelings that had surfaced while recalling his relationship with his dad. Jay-Bob knew he had to focus on the task at hand. He was glad this errand would be particularly pleasant.

When Jay-Bob arrived at the Huffmann spread, he was pleased to see only one vehicle remained in the driveway. He recognized it as the compact car often driven by Katie's friends, which probably meant that Betty Huffmann was alone for the time being.

The family hound, a big, drooling golden retriever, bounded up to the deputy's vehicle to greet him. Obviously Jay-Bob was not a stranger on the premises. He reached under the seat of the cruiser and pulled out a dog biscuit. The pooch hopped up and down, eager for the treat. The deputy turned his attention to the house, where he hoped to find a treat as well.

When he reached the door leading to the kitchen, it swung open for him to enter. The smell of country-fried chicken greeted him like a long-lost friend. Jay-Bob scanned the kitchen. Casserole dishes and baked goods—from pies and cakes to muffins and homemade bread—covered every square inch of counter space in the room.

The deputy closed his eyes, stuck his nose up in the air, and soaked up the delicious aromas. He knew he would not leave the house hungry today.

Betty greeted him in the kitchen. She said she would fix a basket of goodies for him to take home. Then she opened a glass-door cupboard, dug through several large folders, and pulled out more than a half-dozen fat spiral notebooks.

"Here you go—just some of Tom's diaries and school journals," she said, plunking them down on the table.

The deputy leafed through the tattered notebooks. He was surprised that Tom was so prolific. They came in all shapes and sizes, but they were stacked in order—the most recent writings on top and the oldest on the bottom.

"They go back to eighth grade," Betty said. "I marked several of the entries with Post-It notes, but I didn't read it all. You'll see he's been talking about killing his dad for years, though." She put her hand on the stack. "You'll be shocked. There's some really good, juicy plots in there. Tom did not hold much back."

"Thanks," he said. "Guess I've got some reading to do."

"When you bring the warrant out, I'll have the rest of them for you." Betty moved away from the table, ready to reveal more information. "Also got a bunch of screenshots from Facebook. Tom posted comments about his dad on other sites, plus his friends had some real nasty things to say. They talked about cutting his dad up into little pieces and spreading him around the farm."

The deputy nodded, looking down at Betty standing just a few feet away. He smiled and drew her close with one arm. Then he kissed her fully on the lips, opening his mouth slightly for her eager tongue.

"You're the best, Sweet Cheeks," he said, pulling back and looking into her eyes. "Missed you, you know."

"Missed you too," Betty said, her voice low and sultry. "Lord, I love you, Ace."

That made his putter flutter.

They kissed again, letting their lips linger for several minutes.

"Can hardly wait to see you again, but we probably should steer clear of each other for a while," he said. "Let me know when the coast is clear for us to meet."

Jay-Bob moved toward the door, but they held hands until he stepped out into the cold air, heading for his patrol car and back to Bad Axe.

Chapter 14

When Nick arrived in the newsroom Monday morning, he was greeted by the C-Man, who had two messages for him: good work, great copy, and excellent weekend stories; and the editor-in-chief is pissed and wants to see you at nine o'clock.

The reporter thanked Clapper for the compliment and asked what he had done to get the editor's panties all bunched up.

"You shouldn't have ditched the intern last week," the managing editor said, pushing a stack of old newspapers into a portable recycling bin. "You knew Morton had a special connection to Gordon, and you left him while out on assignment."

"Yeah, but the kid is a jerk who does not appreciate the opportunity he's been given—on a silver platter, I might add," Nick said. "He was playing instead of working on the assignment, so I simply left when the work was completed."

Nevertheless, the C-Man said, Morton Reynolds had ordered Nick to report to his office for the morning meeting.

Nick nodded and asked if the managing editor had time to follow up on the ice-fishing death from the weekend. For that day's edition, Nick had written a combination news story and obituary, complete with a nice portrait of Carl Huffmann. He had some ideas for new stories, but he wanted to confer with his boss before getting started.

"I want to talk to the sheriff's department deputy handling the accident and the Huron County medical examiner," Nick said. "Plus, I still haven't spoken with the survivor since Saturday night—would love to spend some time with him when he's up for it. Survivor interviews are always good. Nothing like getting a harrowing experience from one who was there."

Clapper agreed with Nick, but he had a couple of ideas he wanted to chase too, he said. "I'd like a story about the allure and dangers of ice fishing," he told Nick. "This is something we go through every winter."

The editor recounted a long list of instances where rescue crews, including the Coast Guard, had been called into action to save outdoor enthusiasts who'd wandered into harm's way. He noted how often the rescuers put themselves in danger to help individuals who had engaged in dangerous recreational activities.

"Let's do something comprehensive for our readers—hit it from all angles," Clapper said. "Give me perspective from the men and women out there fishing as well as what the rescuers and emergency personnel have to say. Plus the history and tradition of ice fishing—a complete package."

Nick tossed his notebook on his desk. "Tall order, Drayton— that's going to take some doin'," he said. "The cop's report and the ME's assessment will be pretty routine, but you're asking for a lot with the rest of it."

"That's why I'm giving you some help," the C-Man said. He moved around to the other side of his desk, watching for Nick's reaction. "Greta Norris is going to go with you and give you a hand. Called her first thing this morning. She's looking forward to it."

The news delighted Nick. He had worked with Greta on a package of stories related to a Mackinac Island death which had turned out to be a murder. Greta was young, but she had proven herself smart and gritty—a real hustler who loved chasing a tough story almost as much as he did.

As the editor and Nick discussed the scope of the stories they would pursue, Greta whisked into the newsroom. She looked like she was ready for a reindeer roundup at the North Pole. A full-length down-filled parka with fuzzy trim on its hood, snowmobile pants and boots, and insulated vinyl gloves completed her gear. Hot-pack hand warmers poked out of her side pockets.

"Well, how do I look?" she said, holding her hands up to her shoulders and twirling around. "I'm ready to take on Wild Fowl Bay. Let's hit it."

Nick laughed and nodded his approval. "You bet, right after I meet with the editor. Give me ten minutes."

By now the *Blade* newsroom buzzed with activity. Copy editors and reporters worked feverishly to finish the first edition as their morning deadline approached. Phones screamed for attention. Tempers got as overcooked as the break room coffee—lots of shouting among frazzled professionals.

Nick checked the mail on his desk, then gave his watch a quick glance. Meeting with the editor-in-chief, also referred to as the Worm among the reporters, would be painful, but hopefully quick, he thought.

The reporter remembered the day Morton had asked him to take the intern along to interview victims of a tornado that had whisked through the area. The twister had bounced from trailer park to trailer park, tossing the boxlike houses around as if they were tin cans.

Potentially, great experience for any young reporter—talk to people about their brush with the twister, then tell readers about it in an exciting, fast-paced narrative. Except to get a good story, a reporter has got to do the legwork—conduct the interviews, talk with the people affected, and connect with experts to dig out the information that good, detailed reporting requires.

But all that somehow escaped Morton's Golden Boy, who had dismissed the tips that Nick gave him when they first arrived at the scene. The young intern, son of a local bank president who was a golfing buddy of Morton's, had spent all his time drinking Mountain

Dew and eating donuts in the emergency responders' tent. So when Nick finished gathering information to write the story, he'd gone back to the newsroom without the kid.

Since then, the fallout for Nick had been harsh. The Worm had sent him a scathing email detailing his transgression. Then a printed version of the written spanking was hand-delivered by the editor's secretary.

Worst of all, Nick thought, was that the C-Man had taken a tongue-lashing from the editor-in-chief. Additionally, the publisher, D. McGovern Givens, had received a special memo about the misbehavior. But Nick wasn't concerned about what the publisher thought. She had sexually harassed Nick and gotten caught, and now she was impotent when it came to disciplining him.

At 8:50 a.m., Nick headed for the Worm's office, hoping to get it over with and get on the road.

No such luck. Reynolds sat back in his chair, his fingers intertwined and resting on his large, soft belly. He waved for Nick to enter, offering him a seat.

"Do you know why you're here, Nick?" the editor asked.

"Only heard from the C-Man that you wanted to see me," Nick said, not wanting to reveal too much. He leaned back too and crossed his legs. "Thought you might have something interesting to share on cold-water drownings or ice rescues, maybe a story or two about ice fishing yourself."

The editor looked puzzled. He sat forward, placing his elbows on the desk.

"You saw the stories from the weekend about the ice-fishing fatality?" Nick asked. "A man died, and his son nearly lost his life out on the big water. Front-page stories with photos for Sunday, and good follow-up pieces for today's paper."

Still no reaction from the editor other than his blank, empty expression. Obviously Reynolds hadn't read the Sunday paper or what was being published today.

"Ah yes, Nick. Really good stuff," Reynolds said. "But let's get down to what's really important. I want to talk with you about leaving Gordon out on assignment. Very poor judgment and decision-making on your part, Nick."

Reynolds picked up his day planner and flipped through the pages, aloof and distracted. He did not look the reporter in the eye. "Shows a lack of teamwork. Why, that young intern might have gotten lost at the scene—or he might have gotten hurt while under your care and guidance."

Nick tried not to get agitated, but he had no intention of being a babysitter for anybody's golden boy.

"The only thing that would have hurt him out there was eating too many donuts," Nick said. "But I don't think that would have happened, because the Red Cross guys on duty would have stopped him as soon as they saw that big sugar ring around his mouth. What a poor excuse for a reporter!"

"Now, Nick, there you go, getting negative again," the editor said. "I'm afraid there's going to be a penalty for your poor behavior and attitude."

"Why are you defending Gordon?" Nick asked. "He has no writing skills, and his reporting instincts are, well, nonexistent. He's lazy and, quite frankly, not very smart."

The editor did not respond. He took a long sip of his coffee and let the question pass like he usually did when it came to any kind of confrontation.

"Too bad for the young reporter who did not get the internship," Nick said. He had thought the young man very talented—a real go-getter. "But he grew up in a mobile home park in Kawkawlin with his single mom." Nick added that the kid had worked three jobs all the way through college to position himself for a shot at an internship at a daily newspaper. "He wasn't the child of a banker who could toss his weight around to get the advantage for his son."

Nick recalled the rumors that the kid's dad had helped Morton get no-interest financing when he'd bought his new home. The bank had okayed the unusual mortgage and then kept it in-house as a special favor to the editor.

Nick could not let it go. He asked the editor if the story was true.

"I don't deal in rumors, but I will say that Gordon's dad was very kind to me when I first came to Bay City," the Worm said. "I felt like I owed him this favor. It's an internship, not a full-time job. Just wanted to help the young man out."

He sipped his coffee and picked at a sticky bun. After a few minutes he looked up at Nick with a sudden grin, one that said he'd just gotten away with eating a stolen pie. Nick recognized it immediately—it meant Morton had come up with the perfect solution to Nick's misdeed.

"I will let you redeem yourself by taking the intern out with you to the Thumb when you do your follow-ups on that ice adventure, or whatever it was."

Nick's mouth hung agape. "Oh no," he said, trying to come up with the correct words to protest this vast injustice. His mind raced to find good, solid reasoning why coupling him and the intern on assignment wouldn't work.

"Too late," Nick said. "The C-Man already assigned Greta. She's down in the newsroom dressed like one of Santa's helpers—ready to go."

"Drayton can find another story for Greta," Reynolds said. "This will be good for both of you. I expect you to be the best mentor in the world, Nick. Do it as if your job depends on it."

The veiled threat did not escape Nick, but he had been fired before, so it had only a glancing impact. Nick simply did not want to work with a lazy reporter and feared it would get him in more trouble.

"And it will be good for the kid," the Worm said. "He needs to kick up his game a notch or two, and you're just the reporter who can help him."

Reynolds dismissed Nick before he could argue further. The reporter returned to the newsroom and found the intern in the break room, eating donuts.

"Come on," Nick said, jerking his head toward the newsroom. "Hope you've got a warm coat and some insulated gloves." He grabbed his notebook, recorder, and heavy coat as he headed for the door.

"Wow, Nick, are we going out on that big drowning over the weekend?" Gordon asked, licking his fingers. He hurried after the reporter. "This is going to be fun. I can hardly wait."

"Me too," Nick said. "Me too."

Chapter 15

Jay-Bob sat at his desk in the squad room of the Huron County Sheriff's Department, flipping through one of Tom Huffmann's journals. The fat spiral notebook dated from the young man's junior year in high school.

Each page of the journal told a different story about Tom's life. Some pages were sketches or diagrams. Others contained simple doodles, the kind a kid might make while he talked on his phone or listened to music. But most entries were long, personal ramblings on a wide range of topics—from school to buddies and girlfriends to sports to favorite tunes to the farm.

The notebook also contained more than two dozen observations on Tom's family, most of them rants about his dad. Betty Huffmann had used sticky notes to mark the entries where Tom had declared his desire to kill his father. On the first she'd written "Ace, you got to read this one!"

He did. It was a four-page entry with sketches in the margins: stickmen hanged by the neck, stabbed to death with bloody daggers, shot down in a hail of gunfire, or tortured with live electrical wires.

The text was not much better. The deputy read the whole thing and shook his head. It was apparently a narrative Tom had written after waking from a bad dream: "Had night sweats—woke up pounding the old man with both fists. The bastard got drunk and beat my mom again. I was just a little kid, but I jumped on his back and swung as hard as I could. He hurt my mom—and that was the moment I knew I wanted to kill him."

Jay-Bob worked through a few more pages until he found

another sticky note from Betty: "No wonder the kid is touched. This would make anybody a little nutso." No drawings of dead stickmen here—just "DIE, DIE, DIE" written repeatedly in bold capital letters and underlined in red ink, covering every open space on the page.

The entry itself was just one page of text. "I wake up each morning aching to kill my dad. I hate him with every molecule in my body. Since I turned 8, he has ridiculed and humiliated me every single day. If I don't jump right out of bed when he wakes me to do chores, he dumps my mattress and me on the floor, calling me a lazy Lame Brain. He says his belt is my friend and gets it out every time he thinks I screwed up. One of these days I'm going to have a surprise for him. Would love to strangle him with that strap."

The deputy put down the notebook. Carl Huffmann had tortured his son mentally and physically. Jay-Bob wondered how a jury would see it. It was a good thing he'd skipped breakfast, he thought, or he would be hurling in the men's room now. "Sick! Sick! Sick!" he said aloud, almost without thinking.

"Who's sick?" a nearby deputy asked him.

Jay-Bob stood up from his desk and nodded at his fellow lawman. "Sometimes this job just makes you shake your head at the way people treat each other. Hard to swallow."

The squad room around him now percolated with activity. Deputies hustled to put together reports before their shifts started or ended for the day. Jay-Bob needed to read more from Tom's diaries and journals, but he'd had enough for one sitting. It was clear to him that sifting through the volume of written material was going to be difficult. But the job had to be done before he made a recommendation to the prosecutor, asking for criminal charges to be filed against Tom Huffmann.

The phone on his desk rang—the Fairview Township fire chief

was on the line. He asked Jay-Bob to come to his office.

"I'm really tied up here in the squad room doing paperwork from the weekend," the deputy said, leaning back in his swivel chair. "What have you got? Is it something that can wait?"

"Well, sure, it could wait," the chief said. "But you're going to want to see this, and you're probably going to want to see it right away—at least that would be my guess."

Now he had Jay-Bob's attention—and his curiosity. "What the hell is it?"

"A fourteen-inch crescent wrench, found out on the ice not too far from where we pulled up that body yesterday," the chief said. "My guys found it floating on a big chunk of ice. They noticed it because the sea gulls were dive-bombing the thing."

"No kidding. So what attracted the flying rats?"

"Skin," the chief said. He cleared his throat, like he knew Jay-Bob would want more information. "When the guys picked it up, they found a big chunk of skin and some hair stuck in the mechanism that adjusts the size of the wrench. Nasty, but very interesting."

Jay-Bob lost his balance and tipped backward in his chair, hitting the floor with enough noise to draw the attention of every person in the squad room. One of the other deputies shouted an offer of help: "Boog, what the hell is going on? You been drinkin' already this morning?"

The deputy jumped to his feet and picked up his chair, ignoring the hoots and hollers. He had not lost control of the telephone receiver in his clumsy fall. "No shit," he said to the chief. "Did you put that in your report?"

"Yup—all documented."

"I'll be right there to pick it up."

Chapter 16

Nick and the intern made a left turn off M-25 onto Filion Road, heading for the public access to Wild Fowl Bay that runs along Mud Creek. Pickup trucks, many with trailers for snowmobiles or 4-wheelers, sat empty and quiet, parked on both sides of the road. Ice fishers passed one another, some on their way out to try their luck and a few returning to shore. Some hauled coolers spilling over with fresh fish from the bay.

Nick's classic Firebird, with its big, growling V-8 and rear-wheel drive powertrain, seemed out of place. Nonetheless, they motored, windows down, to the end of the road, where the bay stretched out as far as the eye could see.

On the drive up, Nick and Gordon had mapped out their plan for the day. The veteran reporter did not like the idea of working with the intern, but he was determined to make the best of it. Nick would leave the young reporter at the Mud Creek access to interview ice anglers about their sport, its inherent dangers, and why they loved it so.

While the kid worked out on the ice, Nick would drive another forty minutes to Bad Axe, where he hoped to meet with the county medical examiner, the sheriff, and members of the county's cold-water rescue team.

The reporter had also planned to speak with Tom Huffmann about his ordeal and survival. But earlier a spokesperson for Scheurer Hospital had told Nick that Huffmann had been discharged that morning. The reporter would have to locate the survivor and connect another time.

Gordon climbed out of the Firebird and put on his cold-weather gear, which he had peeled off during the ride. He checked his pockets for his handheld voice recorder, a cell phone for photos, and a notebook and pencils. Nick had insisted on the latter, since ink pens tended to freeze.

The intern waved toward the people coming and going at the access. "I shouldn't have any trouble finding anglers," he said. "But I also want to go out on the ice to talk to people while they are fishing. I want to experience it before I try to write about it."

Nick thought that was a very good idea. He was surprised—and delighted—that Gordon was taking the assignment seriously and thinking it through. At the same time, he wanted to make sure the intern was clear about his job. He suggested that he talk to a diverse group of fishers working on the ice.

"Young, old, men, women—the more viewpoints, thoughts, and experiences, the better your story will be," Nick told the kid. "Get lots of color, lots of stories, including traditions. And plenty of photos—and caption info for the people in the pics."

"Got it, lots of color," Gordon said. "Photos too."

"Just be really careful out there," Nick said, emphasizing each word. He was concerned about Gordon stumbling into trouble because he was so young and, well, green. "It's what they call junk ice because of the freezing and thawing—stay close to shore. And make sure you don't fall into abandoned ice-fishing holes either."

"Yeah, Dad, I'll be careful," the intern said with a dismissive laugh. "Just don't forget about me out here, huh?"

"Wouldn't think of it," Nick said, grinning. He tapped his fingers on the steering wheel, hoping he'd covered everything in his final instructions to the intern. "You can never be too cautious around the big water—winter or summer. People who don't respect the lake often get bitten in the ass by it."

Nick watched Gordon waddle off in his thick insulated pants toward a small group of men who were loading their fishing gear onto a sled. The reporter heard him hail the anglers: "Hey, guys, wait up a minute. Can I talk to you?"

Nick was glad to see the rookie was off to a good start.

He pointed the 'Bird toward Bad Axe, but as he turned onto Caseville Road and headed south, his cell phone rang. It was the fire chief calling, so Nick clicked the speaker button.

"Hi chief, what's happening?"

"I can't say—it's not my place to make a public statement," the chief said. "But I thought I'd give you a heads-up."

"A heads-up about what?" Nick asked. He decided to pull over to the side of the road to focus on the new information it sounded like he was going to receive.

"Again, can't say. But all hell is about to break loose. Talk to the sheriff. I'll tell you what I know after somebody else makes it official."

"Okay, thanks, chief. Appreciate it," Nick said. Whatever was happening, he thought it sounded urgent. He hung up and immediately dialed the sheriff's office. The deputy on front desk duty said the sheriff was out and probably would not be back for the rest of the day.

"What about Deputy Ratchett?" Nick asked. "Is he available to take a call?"

The deputy said he was out too. Nick left messages for both, asking that they return his call.

He had a little better luck with the Huron County Medical Examiner's Office. The secretary said her boss was in the office but tied up. She encouraged the reporter to try back later in the day.

"I'll do better than that," Nick said. He turned the key in the ignition and revved the V-8. "I'm on my way to your office. Can you make an appointment for me or at least hold the ME until I get there?"

She said she would try, but that the physician was up to his eyebrows in patient services. The ME was also the director of the Huron County Health Department, which meant he supervised dozens of professionals who delivered health care to hundreds every day.

Nick figured he would have to catch the ME on the run.

Fortunately for him, as he parked outside the ME's office, a beat-up old Chevy station wagon pulled into the front-row space marked "Reserved for Medical Examiner. Don't even think of parking in this spot." A short, portly man with a handlebar mustache and graying hair, which was parted down the middle so that it lined up perfectly with the space in the 'stache, stepped out of the hulking wreck, talking on his cell phone. The way he rolled and fell to one knee as he got out of his vehicle made Nick think of a Butterball turkey. The rotund medical doctor reached back into the bulky wagon and pulled out a large black satchel.

The reporter reached him before he could lock up his vehicle. Nick had to wonder what was in the wagon, because the rusting boat itself was not worth stealing.

"Hi Doc, I'm Nick Steele from *The Bay City Blade*," he said. "Could I talk with you for a few minutes while we walk to your office?"

"Sure, but you got to make it quick." The doctor clicked off his cell phone and stuck it in the breast pocket of his navy blue pinstripe vest. "You're probably here about the drowning Sunday."

"You already determined he drowned?" Nick asked.

"Man's lungs were filled with water—that's drowning," the doc said. "Very sad to see."

"Anything else noteworthy?" Nick had to walk quickly to keep up with the medical man, who was moving a lot faster than the reporter thought possible. "Everything else routine, what you expected?"

"Had a cut on his forehead, right at the eyebrow and extending back toward his temple," the doc said, reaching for his cell phone, which beckoned again.

"A cut? What from, could you tell?" Nick jumped in front of the ME as he stopped to answer his phone.

"A blow to the head," the doc said. The cell buzzed. "The man had just taken a dive in ten feet of water while riding a two thousand-pound machine. Handlebars? One of the fenders? Back tail rack? Could be a lot of things. But Huffmann got the cut before drowning—that's clear."

The ME answered his phone and turned away from Nick so he could speak privately. But the call only took a few moments, and the doc told Nick that he had to run. "Got a grieving family that's been waiting all morning to see me," he said.

"One final question, Doc. Was the injury to his head severe enough to kill him?"

The doc shook his head. "Might have dazed him or knocked him out, but water in the lungs is what killed him." He turned to leave. "Gotta go. It will all be in my final report."

The ME hustled away and disappeared into the government building. Nick headed back into Bad Axe to visit the sheriff's department. He hoped to connect with the sheriff or Deputy Ratchett. The new information about the injury to Carl Huffmann was interesting, he thought, and it made him remember the cement-filled pipe again. He decided to call Nora Thompson to see if she had heard anything new from Tom Huffmann.

Nice Nurse Nora was delighted to hear from Nick. She told him she had visited Tom in the hospital late Sunday afternoon, and that he was doing well physically but suffering emotionally; Nora thought he might be depressed.

"I think everything that happened kinda caught up to him all at once," she told Nick, who listened intently. He figured the nurse was his best connection to Tom and his best hope of interviewing the tragic accident's lone survivor. "On the one hand, he was glad—and maybe even a little surprised—that he was alive and recovering. But on the other hand, he had been through an exhaustive ordeal, and he'd lost his father."

"Did any of that strike you as unusual?" Nick asked. "Wouldn't that be expected?"

Nora agreed that it would. She said Tom seemed down, very blue, but that he could not thank her and her family enough for their assistance and support. The two had exchanged contact information, she said, and agreed to stay in touch.

"Tom said I reminded him of his birth mother," Nora said. "He told me he had not felt such comfort since his mother passed away."

"Wow, Nora, that's very nice," Nick said. "Sounds like you had a profound effect on Tom. I'll bet that made you feel good."

"It did," she said. But a hint of alarm in her voice told Nick that something was bothering her. He hoped she'd reveal it.

Nora took a deep breath. "But then he said something that caught me so off guard, I didn't know how to respond."

"What's that?"

"He said he missed his mother, and he was glad his old man was dead." Nora paused, as though she wasn't sure how Nick would react to what had Tom told her. "I didn't say anything—just stood there looking at him, trying to figure out if he was serious or if it was an attempt at humor, a bad joke."

He asked Nora how she'd gauged the comment.

The nurse said Tom had repeated the remark, telling her it was a long story and a complicated one. He said he was going to spend some time with his brother in Bay City, and that he would call her when he'd had time to sort things out.

Nick thanked Nora and checked his watch. He wondered how Gordon was doing back at Mud Creek. The intern had been there nearly three hours, and Nick hoped he was okay. Lots can happen in a few hours, and he was concerned about the kid being unsupervised that long. He hoped he could make a fast connection at the sheriff's department.

The parking lot of the sheriff's department was packed. But most of the vehicles, Nick knew, belonged to visitors checking on inmates. He wouldn't know if the sheriff or Deputy Ratchett were available until he inquired.

Inside the building, Nick made straight for the front desk deputy, who was handling a phone call. She stood behind a long desk with a plexiglass window above it. A door at the end of the window had no handle on the outside. The rest of the room behind her was empty except for Ratchett, who sat at his desk, reading a spiral notebook. The deputy did not look up.

Nick waved both hands over his head, trying to get Ratchett's attention, but all the maneuver did was annoy the front desk deputy. She shook her head and frowned at Nick through the plexiglass. Nick waved his hands again.

"Can you hold on just a second?" the deputy said into her phone. "I got a guy out here who's jumping up and down like he's going to wet his pants."

She rested the phone on her shoulder and pushed the window sideways, addressing Nick in a harsh, curt tone.

"Just trying to get Deputy Ratchett's attention," he said. "Didn't mean to interrupt you. Is he available or still tied up?"

She held up her hand like a traffic cop on the street. "Booger, you got a visitor!" she shouted over her shoulder toward the back of the squad room. "He's a pushy one. You want him to come back, or you gonna come up?"

Jay-Bob looked up from the notebook, recognized Nick, and said he would be right out.

"Did you just call him Booger?" Nick asked.

"Pretend you didn't hear me," the deputy said. "He don't like being called that, especially by strangers. He prefers Ace."

Nick nodded just as Jay-Bob pushed open the door next to the window. "Howdy. Whatcha need?" He held the door with one arm and a foot, like he didn't expect the conversation to take long.

"Looking for an update on the drowning," Nick said. "Can you give me a few minutes?"

"You were there." Jay-Bob shrugged. He gave Nick a look that said that was the end of the story. "Not much more to tell you. Body was recovered. Victim who survived is still in hospital, last I heard."

"His brother picked him up, so he's been discharged," Nick said. He hoped offering Jay-Bob a bit of new information would get the deputy to reciprocate. "Just talked with the ME, who mentioned that the drowning victim had been injured before he died. Wondered if we could talk about that."

Jay-Bob hesitated and pulled back from the door. "I'm not authorized to talk about it," he said. "Any new information regarding the injury will have to come from the sheriff. I figure he'll issue a press release if he's got anything to say."

Nick nodded. He said he understood. The reporter handed the deputy his card, asking Jay-Bob to give it to the sheriff. "I'll be in the area all afternoon. Would love to talk with him—even if he can't speak about the gash on the victim's head."

"Who said anything about a gash?" The deputy seemed surprised by how much Nick knew. Information was like gold, and neither man wanted to give away too much of it.

"I did," Nick said. "Just got that from the ME, who was gracious enough to give me a few minutes even though he's busy as a hound dog checking rabbit holes."

Jay-Bob grunted and grinned. "I will make sure I pass it along."

"Say, Deputy, one more thing that I think I should mention to you." The reporter figured the timing was right to talk about the pipe he'd spotted at the Thompson cottage. He hoped sharing the info might also break the barrier between him and the deputy. "When I was at the cottage on Sand Point after Tom showed up, I helped the Thompsons clean up the mess—melted ice on the floor and their visitor's soaking-wet clothing.

"Then I found a chunk of pipe filled with cement." Nick held his index fingers about a foot apart and studied the deputy's face to gauge his reaction to the new information. "It was thick and had a cap at one end. Couldn't figure out what it was, so I showed it to Gary Thompson. He thought it might have been used as some kind of tool on the 4-wheelers."

The deputy grunted again, but he asked Nick what had become of the pipe.

The reporter said he'd left it on the bench near the door of the Thompsons' place. "Now that we know Carl Huffmann had a head injury before he died, I thought I should tell someone in authority about it."

If Jay-Bob's ego had gotten a boost from the comment, he didn't show it. "Don't think that chunk of pipe has anything to do with Mr. Huffmann's passing, but I appreciate you mentioning it."

Disappointed that his information was not valued, Nick thanked the deputy and walked over to Main Street, looking for a coffee shop. He was cold and thirsty, but it was too early for a beer.

Coffee Cup Plus was a friendly hangout. The cozy breakfast and lunch shop was long and narrow, forcing customers into close proximity to one another. No secrets in this place. The reporter stepped inside and drew the warm, moist air through his nostrils, savoring the aroma. Obviously, grilled onions were part of the menu. Nick was suddenly hungry.

All the restaurant's tables were full, but the front counter, where a big "Order here" sign hung over the cash register, had a few vacant seats. A man and a woman sat to the side of the counter, chatting over sandwiches and coffee. The man wore a polo shirt and khaki pants, but the woman was dressed in a sheriff's department uniform. Nick stood in the order line as close to the couple as possible.

The line moved as slowly as a clock approaching quitting time. The pair sitting near Nick, probably in their mid-forties and too friendly and cordial to be married, talked shop. They didn't seem sappy and mushy enough to Nick to be romantic partners, though, and he suspected friends with benefits. The woman, Nick figured, was a jail guard who supervised female inmates. It sounded like Khaki Pants worked in the prosecutor's office, shuffling records.

The guard leaned sideways to talk quietly with her friend. "Heard that drowning on Sunday wasn't exactly accidental."

Nick tried to act casual while inching closer.

Khaki Pants licked the mayonnaise squishing out between his fingers. "What do you mean?" he said. "That guy went into the water at nighttime. It would have been a miracle if he'd survived."

"You didn't hear this from me"—she dropped her voice so low that Nick had to scoot in close to keep her audible—"but they think they may have found a weapon."

"A weapon?" The man's reply was so loud, the guard swatted him on the arm and gave him a look that would have melted iron. Nick leaned back and pretended to look away. Khaki Pants glanced around the coffee shop, then lowered his voice to a whisper. "It was a father and son out there. Why would there be a weapon?"

"Shh. Don't know," she said. "Only heard they found a weapon with evidence on it—some kind of human tissue."

Nick could barely contain himself. He wanted to ask questions, a bunch of them, but did not dare step into the conversation. By now the line to place orders had moved him closer to the register and out of range of the gossip at the counter.

But he was no longer hungry. He ordered a large coffee to go, and headed for the exit.

Across the street, alongside the sheriff's department and jailhouse, stood the county courthouse, which housed the prosecutor's office. The reporter stepped into the street, waiting for a double-trailer sugar beet truck to rumble past. He needed to reach Gordon. If Nick could verify what he'd heard at the coffee shop, he knew they'd have a great story to write, and he wanted the rookie to be ready to chase it. He sent the young reporter a text message: "Story may be taking a turn. Need to connect. Still at Mud Creek access?"

Nick entered the lobby of the courthouse and found a sign directing him to the prosecutor's office on the lower level, which was dimly lit and musty. District and circuit courts, as well as the probation office, were all located in the basement of the building.

The receptionist informed him that none of the legal beagles were available. Someone, she said, would be back before the end of the day.

Nick thanked her. He looked around the room and sniffed the air. "Say, just curious—what's that pervasive musty smell? Is there a moisture problem down here?"

The receptionist put her hands on her hips and gave Nick a look that he interpreted as exasperation. "No moisture problem. That's the smell of poverty. Go out in the hall and take a look at who's sitting there waiting for court or probation. Poor people, most of whom got absolutely nothing, and they end up here."

The salty response surprised Nick. He left his card and asked that the prosecutor or one of the assistants give him a call.

As he pushed open the door, his cell phone dinged with a text from Gordon. "Just left Mud Creek, got some great stuff! Hitched a ride on a snowmobile to the Bluewater Inn in Caseville. Catch you later."

Nick shook his head and grimaced. He waited a few minutes before responding. Nick's instincts told him the story was about to take a dramatic turn—and he wanted to be on top of it when it did, not chasing an intern around a bar full of ice fishermen, farmers, and malcontents.

"Okay, coming to pick you up. We gotta fly!" Nick texted. He headed to Caseville, hoping to catch Gordon before he got in over his head.

Chapter 17

Tom Huffmann opened the door to his brother Richard's refrigerator. Cold cuts and cheese overflowed from the meat tray. A wild assortment of plasticware bulged with leftovers—some of it green and furry looking. The top shelf and the door were loaded with cold bottles of beer. Tom studied the contents for several minutes, shook his head in disdain at the biology experiment gone horribly bad, and then grabbed two frosty beers.

"Are you making dinner in there or getting us a couple of cold ones?" Richard said, his voice raised so he could be heard from the next room. "I'm thirsty. Bring the beers so we can toast the old man."

Tom carried the brews to Richard's living room, where his brother was stretched out on the couch. "You know you got the makings of a bio-disaster brewing in your fridge? Come on, man, you gotta clean once in a while."

A decade separated Richard and Tom in age. The brothers had only become close in the last few years, though the two shared the Huffmann receding hairline, dark eyes, general size, and reluctant smile. There the similarities stopped. Richard, who had become an accountant, was proud to be a city guy. He had never taken to farm work, especially with his dad, and had left home soon after high school.

Now Richard lived in one of the new condo developments in downtown Bay City. The condo had been his home since Wife #2 bailed on him just over a year before, and the place was decorated in low-end garage sale items—hard-up bachelor motif. Though the living room was small, it had a sliding glass door that led to a balcony overlooking the Saginaw River, which split Bay City into its east and west sides.

"Here's to Carl, the dirty bastard," Richard said, lifting his Killian's to clink it with Tom's. A big smile creased Richard's face. He raised his brew higher in the air as a salute. "May he finally find peace."

"Yeah, and then may he rot in hell," Tom said. The brothers laughed and sipped heavily at their beers.

Silence fell over the living room. Richard put his drink down and walked to the balcony door, opening it slightly. Cold air rushed into the room, chilling it despite the warm sunshine outside.

Without turning to face his brother, he asked the question that had been eating at him since Saturday night, when he'd received word of the accident on the ice.

"So, Tom, did you kill him?" Richard stuck his head out the balcony door and watched a few ice fishermen working the edge of the river, staying clear of the shipping channel, which was about thirty feet deep. "Wouldn't blame you if you did," he said. "Believe me, I thought about it plenty of times."

Tom joined his brother at the balcony door. Richard wondered if the sight of the anglers would make him anxious, but Tom didn't turn away. He took another long pull of the bottle of Killian's.

"I won't lie to you," Tom said, leaning against the doorframe. "I went out on the ice with every intention of taking the old man down, but I couldn't do it. I even made a club to whack him over the head. But every time I got ready, he started talking about Mom and the old days—Christmas, birthdays, harvest and planting seasons."

"Made you think about all the good times, right?" Richard snorted. "Problem is, there were too damn few good times and a whole lot of miserable ones. With that SOB, the bad far outweighed the good." He motioned for Tom to join him over at the dining table, then pulled out a chair.

What Richard was more interested in was the farm. He wanted to know what Tom planned to do with it, and how long before his younger brother could buy out his interest. Their brother Bill would want a buyout too, he knew.

"You going to keep working the farm, or you planning to sell it?" Richard asked. "Got to be five or six million bucks in land, and maybe a couple more in equipment. I'm thinking we should get a professional appraisal of everything, and then you can divide it up fair and square." He waited for a response. Certainly, he thought, Tom would have considered what would become of the farm after their dad's death—his brother had had a lot of time to think since he'd wandered off the ice without his old man.

Tom sipped his beer and nodded at Richard. He seemed surprised that his brother had thought so far ahead. "Gonna need to talk with the family attorney and the accountant so we do it smart," he said, promising he would map out a plan of action after the funeral. "Don't want to pay a nickel more in taxes than we have to."

Going slow was not the answer Richard had been hoping to hear. He retrieved his beer and nursed it for a few minutes to let the words settle. Then he moved to the other side of the living room.

"Sooner the better, as far as Bill and I are concerned," he said. "No point in dragging this out so the lawyer and accountant can run up their fees. We want to do a little traveling, see the world some, and we'll need a few bucks to do that."

Tom said nothing. Richard flipped on the basketball game, and for a few minutes they watched the Lakers give the Pistons a pounding on TV. Then he muted the volume to ask Tom about his relationship with Betty. Richard was curious whether they'd discussed money and the farm—another question that seemed to catch Tom off guard.

"First thing you're going to have to do is get that witch and her bitch daughter off the property," Richard said. "It's a good thing the old man insisted on that prenup before they got hitched. You shouldn't have any trouble moving her out, and the quicker the better for all of us."

Tom nodded. He said that was why he had not returned to the farmhouse after being discharged from the hospital. He told Richard he didn't want to see Betty after they buried his dad, and would not stay in the house with her and her daughter on the premises. "She will be out the day after the funeral," Tom said. "Already put her on notice when she came to the hospital. Didn't say a word, just stood there smiling when I told her."

Silence fell over the condo. Tom stared at the floor as if he expected to find answers in the carpeting. The quiet became uncomfortable, almost stifling. Finally Richard turned on his stereo system, and the condo filled with the sweet melodies of the Rev. Al Green in "How Can You Mend a Broken Heart?"

"I'll tell you what, I thought we were both goners out there on that bay," Tom said, still boring holes into the carpet. "Out in that cold-ass water, when we couldn't touch the bottom, I kept thinking, 'This is it, this is it. It's over. We're not going to make it.'

"But the old man kept his head. He kept saying, 'Keep movin', don't stop. We're goin' to make it. Come on, keep going.' When we hit a sandbar, the old man pushed me up onto the ice, and then I pulled him out. But that shit didn't last," Tom said. He watched his brother, who was focused on each word. "First thing we knew, he'd broken through in another bad spot. He told me to keep going. He was going to find the sandbar so he could get back out. Never saw him again. Last thing I heard him say was 'Follow those Christmas tree lights. Keep going till you get there.'"

Tom put his head in his hands, leaning forward until the back of his hands touched his knees. Then he cried, bawling like a hungry calf. Richard held his shoulders while the younger man trembled, his whole body shaking gently. Al Green crooned the opening lines of "Let's Stay Together."

Richard spoke to his brother in a voice so soft it could barely be heard. "It's okay, you made it. There's a reason for that. You're supposed to pick up and move on from here. All we've got is each other now. We've just got to keep moving, keep going, knowing that we're going to make it."

Richard tried to comfort his brother, but he couldn't help thinking about his inheritance too. If he and Bill were going to get their hands on it soon, Tom would have to pull himself together.

Chapter 18

By Monday morning, the death on Wild Fowl Bay had become the center of office gossip among hundreds of employees killing time and burning up taxpayer dollars in Huron County public offices.

The Huffmanns were well-known across the Upper Thumb, and most folks had their own theories about the family and what had happened on the ice covering Wild Fowl Bay. The gossip, which raged like wildfire, ranged from conspiracy rhetoric to religious cleansings to cult worship. Nothing, it seemed, was too crazy or harebrained to be ruled out.

Preston Billington, Huron County prosecutor, had been alerted Sunday morning when Carl Huffmann's body was snagged by a sheriff's deputy in an eighteen-foot fishing boat. At that time, the common belief was that a terrible accident had claimed one of the Huffmanns' lives and seriously threatened the other.

Now a simple accident had gotten messy. Deputy Jay-Bob Ratchett was standing in Billington's office asking for murder charges, a horse of a whole different color. Billington knew that a crescent wrench with skin and hair stuck to it had just been sent off to the Michigan State Police crime lab for complete analysis. But apparently Jay-Bob had already concluded that the wrench had been Tom Huffmann's weapon. As far as the deputy was concerned, Tom had knocked his father unconscious, then finished him off by drowning his dad in the frigid waters of Saginaw Bay.

Billington had recently been re-elected to a second term in office, but it was by the slimmest of margins. After surviving a recount, he operated on the idea that he had little room for error when deciding which crimes brought before him could be prosecuted and won. Additionally Billington had picked up his share of enemies in the county government. For example, Jay-Bob's boss, the county sheriff, could not stand the sight of the prosecutor. They enjoyed sniping at each other as if they were sharpshooters in a war-torn country. Billington never missed a chance to humiliate the sheriff in front of the county board of commissioners as well as the judges and courthouse personnel. The sheriff was no better, often going out of his way to make the prosecutor look like a fool and a boob.

That's why the deputy had taken his theory directly to the prosecutor rather than have the county's top cop ask for charges to be filed. This delighted Billington, who saw it as an opportunity to make some political hay while taking the lead in a potentially explosive murder plot.

"What else have you got?" Billington said, running his long, bony fingers through his thinning gray hair. The prosecutor was tall and lanky, except for the large potbelly upon which he often rested his folded hands. He wore a brown corduroy suit, which was wearing thin at the elbows, knees, and seat.

"No witnesses, of course," Jay-Bob said, sitting on the corner of the prosecutor's desk. "But I have reason to believe evidence can be found at the Huffmann farmhouse."

"What kind of evidence?"

"Written documents in Tom Huffmann's own handwriting where he specifically vows to kill his father," Jay-Bob said. "I understand there's a pile of it at the farm."

"What else?" Billington liked where the information was heading, but he wanted a mountain of evidence. He did not want to take this case in front of a jury unless it was a slam-dunk conviction.

"Indications are strong that Tom talked with, and perhaps conspired with, friends about killing his father." The deputy reached into his satchel, which was brimming with spiral notebooks, and pulled out his laptop. "We have written evidence, some of it posted on the internet, social media—discussions with friends."

The deputy grinned in apparent satisfaction at his investigative work. "Here you go—take a look at these posts from Facebook and Snapchat," Jay-Bob said. "It will give you a chill and make your hair stand on end."

Boney Fingers opened the laptop. The computer whirred to life, and an image popped up on its large screen. The prosecutor winced, then scrunched his face up in disgust and shook his head. "Deputy, this is Pornhub, and it's so raunchy I want to puke."

"What? Oh shit," Jay-Bob said, snatching the laptop back from the prosecutor. He made a series of quick clicks on the keyboard. "There, there you go. Now, that's got it. Here, now you got Facebook and Snapchat posts."

Billington took back the laptop with much trepidation, fearful of what Jay-Bob might spring on him next. "Okay, interesting," he said, skimming the posts and the comments from Tom's friends. After several minutes of review, the prosecutor closed the computer and handed it back to Jay-Bob.

"I'm just trying to think this through," he said. "How is a jury going to react to a bunch of young people chatting on social media? Will the jury see it as youthful banter or damning evidence?"

The deputy nodded in agreement. "Well, that's why we've got to round 'em up and interview them on the record. They're well-known people in the community. Could be good witnesses and good testimony."

"What else? Motive?"

"What else you want?" Jay-Bob asked, standing, which put him nearly face to face with the prosecutor. "He had years of hatred and animosity—I just showed you the proof."

"What about inheritance?" The prosecutor scratched his head and watched the chunks of white, fluffy dandruff float down toward his desk. He brushed it off toward Jay-Bob, who jumped out of the way. "How much money are we talking about here?"

"The Huffmann family is worth millions, but Tom won't get the farm—at least that's what I hear," the deputy said.

Billington nodded. Under Michigan law, the property always went to the wife unless there was legal provision for it to go elsewhere. The prosecutor wanted to find out exactly who was in line to get the farm and the cash before deciding on charges.

He told Jay-Bob he wanted to think about the information that the deputy had brought him. He also would wait for the crime lab analysis. No legal documents would be filed, he said, before the funeral on Wednesday.

In the meantime, he suggested that Jay-Bob and a couple of other deputies interview the young people who'd posted on social media. "Let's see what they've got to say and whether it'll play out in a courtroom at all."

One of the prosecutor's secretaries entered the office without knocking. He carried an armload of folders and held them up in the air. Billington pointed to a clear spot on his desk, where the files landed with a thud.

Jay-Bob waved at the prosecutor as he backpedaled out the door. Then he reached into his jacket for the new disposable cell he'd picked up. The deputy had other sheriff's department business to take care of, but now that he had made a case to the prosecutor, asking for murder charges, the death on Wild Fowl Bay had moved to the top of his priorities list.

Once in the parking lot and out of earshot of others, Jay-Bob made two calls. No answers, so he left identical messages: "On board with PB. He says no warrant until after funeral. More later—only on this cell."

The deputy returned to his desk to pore over the rest of Tom Huffmann's journals and diaries, notebooks that had not yet been subpoenaed and were not supposed to be in his possession. But Jay-Bob needed more evidence, and he hoped the personal writings of the younger Huffmann would yield something solid.

Chapter 19

When Nick entered the Bluewater Inn, the beer chatter stopped as the locals quieted for a chance to size up the stranger in the doorway. They returned to their mugs of brew before Nick's eyes adjusted to the dim lighting in the legendary Caseville bar.

Immediately to his left stood a couple he learned were Shine and Sheila. They occupied their usual position at the end of the eighty-foot bar, nursing drinks. At the opposite end sat Toad and Wart, two old duffers who picked up their nicknames in elementary school based on the myth that warts always appeared wherever toads showed up. They were that close their whole lives. The two were perched like protective bookends on either side of Gordon, the young guy who was supposed to be under Nick's care and guidance.

Gordon did not see Nick right away. His head was buried in the crook of his arm, which rested on the bar's elbow rail. As Nick approached, the kid sat upright on his stool, then stepped around Wart and barreled headfirst into the men's restroom.

Nick acknowledged Toad and Wart, but he could hear the banker's son retching in the men's room. He smiled. He figured it served the kid right—in Nick's experience, drinking shots of straight liquor on an empty stomach never ended well.

"Hi guys, my name is Nick. Gordon, the one hurling his guts out, is my colleague," Nick said, barely able to get out the word "colleague" without doing some retching of his own. He pulled up a chair at a nearby table.

Toad and Wart laughed, a high-pitched cackle that erupted from their throats in unison. They introduced themselves to Nick and said they were keeping an eye on his friend because it was very obvious he was an inexperienced imbiber.

Gordon roared again from the restroom, his agony echoing off tile and porcelain. The accompanying cry of piercing pain was the exclamation point to the old guys' pronouncement that the kid couldn't handle the bar's demon rum.

The Bluewater was about half-full this afternoon, with weekday regulars as well as visitors. Mahogany paneling, dark carpeting, and only a couple of exterior windows gave the bar a dark, foreboding feel. But the clientele was far from somber. A country-western tune by Waylon Jennings twanged from the jukebox. On the bar's other side, three pool tables were in use, with challengers lining up their quarters to take on the champs.

Toad and Wart told Nick that Gordon had rolled into the bar with some ice fishermen who were now playing on the second table. They did not know the names of the anglers. Nick planned to thank the guys for keeping an eye on Gordon once the intern felt good enough to come out of the restroom.

Jill, a blond bartender whose facial expression said, "Don't mess with me or I will crush your nuts into dust," asked Nick if he wanted a drink. The reporter wanted a beer in the worst way but decided against it. Too early in the day, he thought, and he figured he'd best get the kid back to Bay City.

While he waited for Gordon, Nick asked Toad and Wart about the death of the ice fisherman on Wild Fowl Bay. Sometimes the best information comes from folks who live in the area; they are not as worried about being politically or legally correct as the community's so-called officials.

"Damn shame," Wart said.

Toad itched the thinning gray hair on his head, which matched his whiskers in length, thickness, and color. "I met Carl in here—back in his drinking days," he told Nick. "Hadn't seen him in several years, but he always seemed like a good guy."

The men said they'd never met Betty Huffmann—she was not from the area, as far as they knew.

"I remember Carl coming back from a corn seed convention in Des Moines several years ago," Toad said, sipping his Bud Light and leaning on the bar rail. "Said he'd met a sweet gal out there and had invited her to visit. Next thing we heard, a dark-haired beauty was moving into his place."

Nick made a mental note of what they'd said about Betty and how she'd come into the picture. He was glad Dave was looking into her background. Nick asked if the two old-timers were surprised that Carl's son had survived the accident on the ice.

"Boy, that is some wild tale. Hard to figure how he got out of that water and walked to safety," Toad said, pushing himself off the bar rail. He stood to make a point. "A lot of people don't know this, but Wild Fowl Bay is shallow—lots of vegetation on the lake bottom. Very viney and stringy. You get tangled up in the weeds in deeper water with boots and outdoor gear on, and you're really damn lucky if you think you'll get out."

The two men recounted other recent close calls. With the warmer weather, ice fishermen were breaking through all along the coastline of the Thumb, from Sebewaing to Caseville and beyond. The only safe places to fish, they said, were the inland canal systems on Sand Point and some of the local rivers.

Gordon moaned and coughed in the men's room, interrupting the discussion. They heard the toilet flush twice, then the sound of water splashing in the sink, and finally the hand dryer.

Toad leaned over to Nick as if he were telling him a secret. "Gotta say this before the young guy comes out," he said, looking both ways to see if anyone was listening. "Your buddy was loaded when he walked in the door. Also smelled like he got run over by a skunk. I think he was tootin' on some of that wacky tobacky. Really bombed and wobbly. Thought you should know."

Nick thanked Toad just as Gordon emerged from the men's room. The kid had peeled off most of his cold-weather gear, and Nick wondered if he would find Gordon's stuff in a trail leading to the pool tables.

"Hi kid, how you doin'?" he asked.

"Great, couldn't be better." But his words were slurred and his eyes unfocused. "Now, I want you to know that was just the dry heaves in there," Gordon said. "All through college I was known as the King of Heaves. Nobody at CMU was better than me. Lots of noise, but no wash—every time. Go Chips!"

Central Michigan University, long known as one of Michigan's great party colleges, was also recognized for its well-trained journalists—at least those who spent more time writing than retching. Gordon was obviously proud of both his school and his prowess while hugging the porcelain.

"See you met my friends, Toby and Wade," the kid said. "Good guys. They saved me."

"You mean Toad and Wart saved you—from what?"

"Yeah, Toad, Toby, whatever," Gordon said, looking for his wallet, which Wart handed to him after the kid searched for a few minutes. "A fight between the turbine workers and the local guys at the pool tables. And I was right in the middle of it. Scared the hell out of me."

Nick looked at Toad and Wart, who shook their heads, indicating that Gordon had not read the situation correctly. The young reporter said he was going to round up his gear.

When he stepped away, Wart explained. "Young guys. Testosterone overload," he said. "Wasn't much, just huffing and puffing. A little sparring back and forth, mostly loud talk. The Caseville guys don't much care for the City-ots, strangers just here to work on the turbines."

Nick nodded, recognizing human nature for what it was— turf protection. Tossing alcohol into the mix didn't help either, he knew.

Gordon staggered toward the bar, carrying his cold-weather clothing. The intern bumped into a chair, knocking it sideways, then righted himself.

"The guys wanted me to play some more, but I told 'em you were here to take me home," he said, slipping on his parka. He had trouble with the zipper, pulling it closer to his face and leaning down so he could achieve the task, and he almost tipped over again. The kid's slurred speech indicated he was still loaded. "Are we ready to go, Nick?"

Nick waved to Toad and Wart and left Jill a five-spot for putting up with his friend, and the two headed for the exit. The intern wobbled as he stepped into the Firebird, then fell into the seat in a heap.

On their way out of town, the kid mentioned that he'd met a really cool guy who was a collector. But before Gordon could elaborate, he dozed off in his seat, his head rolling back and forth across the headrest.

Nick turned up the music to drown out the snoring and snorting rookie. He had hoped to hear how the interviews went at Mud Creek. Now that the story was developing, he could hardly wait to connect with his girlfriend, Tanya, and Dave to get their takes on how to chase it. He was glad he didn't need to rely on the inebriated intern.

Before long Essexville came into view, the bedroom community east of Bay City and home to a Consumers Power coal-burning plant. The tall smokestacks reminded Nick of the wind turbines he'd just left behind in the Thumb and the clash of old and new tides of energy. It made him wonder if the coal-burning plant had the same kind of impact on families that the turbines were having now. He glanced over at the intern. Still there, still out.

By the time Nick pulled into the employee parking lot at *The Blade*, the rookie was snoring like a lumberjack who'd just finished a twelve-hour shift in the woods. Nick couldn't rouse him. The older reporter covered the younger one with a blanket and tucked it under his chin.

"Now, if you hurl in my Firebird, I'm afraid I'm going to have to end your life," he said, patting the kid on the chest. "And no slobber on my blanket. Never know when I might need it to sleep one off."

Gordon did not respond or move. Nick got out of his beloved ride and locked the door. But before he could enter the building, a silver Cadillac pulled into the parking lot, carrying Morton Reynolds—and his buddy the banker, Gordon's dad.

"Aw shit!" Nick said aloud. He could not believe what was happening. He stuck his head inside the building and asked one of the pressmen to call the newsroom and ask the C-Man to come to the back parking lot. Nick was of the opinion that his managing editor was the only person who could save him now.

The Caddie skidded when the banker spotted his pride and joy in Nick's car. "What the hell is going on here?" the banker said as he jumped out of his vehicle. The kid's face, pressed up against the passenger's side window and contorted as if it were some kind of warped reflection in a carnie's circus mirror, was rather horrifying. Morton rolled out too, fear spreading across their faces as though the two were watching a psycho-slasher movie.

"My boy, my boy," the banker said as he knocked on the side window. The noise and vibration sent the intern rolling sideways in the other direction. The sudden movement also prompted a round of projectile vomiting, covering Nick's center console and splashing chunky orange liquid on the dashboard.

"My god, he's dying in there, Morton! Do something—now!"

The editor ran to his own vehicle and pulled a jack handle out of his trunk. When he got back to the Firebird, the publisher had pulled into the parking lot and joined the banker at the side of Nick's ride. A slight smirk worked the corners of her mouth as she expressed her surprise.

"Well, well. What have we got here?" she said. "Somebody might want to ask Nick for his keys before you go smashing in windows."

That made too much sense. The two men, top executives and supposedly innovative thinkers, looked at each other as if her comment were some kind of scientific breakthrough, or a cure for cancer.

"What? The keys to the car?" Morton said, allowing the jack handle to come down from its striking position. "Ah, good idea."

By now Nick had returned to the scene. He pulled out his keys without a word and opened the passenger's side door. Gordon rolled out into his father's arms, vomit and bile covering his chest and Nick's blanket.

"Somebody call an ambulance, please!" the banker said. "My son is dying."

As attention focused on the current state of Gordon, a crowd of newsroom, advertising, and pressroom personnel had gathered in the parking lot to see what had caused the commotion. Most whispered to each other as they watched the drama. It wasn't often that they had the chance to watch such entertaining antics involving editorial personnel during work hours. Nick's high-wire acts usually occurred around two in the morning, when the bars closed down.

"Don't think he needs an ambulance," Dave Balz said from the crowd, stroking his chin like he was pulling a thousand years of knowledge and experience out of his noggin. "What he needs is sleep, and maybe a shower would help."

Gordon slowly came around as his dad rocked him in his arms. "I swear I will never take another drink as long as I live," he said, struggling to stand on his own.

"Think I've heard that declaration a time or two," Dave said. He covered his mouth to suppress a laugh. "He'll be okay in a day or so. Lots of fluids, and a nice, greasy hamburger after he sleeps some more. That always does it for me."

The banker tossed Nick's blanket in the salty slush of the parking lot and helped his son to the Caddie. Over his shoulder, he told Morton he would call him after he got Gordon home.

The crowd of *Blade* employees, not completely unfamiliar with the wreckage wrought by Satan's favored beverages, slowly dispersed. But Morton, the C-Man, and the publisher stood alongside the Firebird, waiting for some kind of explanation from Nick.

Nick said he'd taken Gordon to his reporting assignment, given him tips and final instructions, and then left him to work on his end of the story. When they reconnected several hours later, he said, he'd discovered that the rookie had been drinking. He did not mention the pot.

"So you left him again," Morton said, his arms crossed over his chest. He tapped his foot on the snow-covered parking lot. "Didn't we just go through this with you, Nick?"

"Wait a minute, wait a minute," Nick said, trying to defend himself to a group of managers who were in no mood for more Nick and Dave hijinks. "I tried to help him, but I can't hold his hand. He's an adult and responsible for his own actions."

Morton looked at the C-Man and said he wanted a full written report on the incident. "In the meantime Nick is suspended, pending further review."

"Really," Nick said. "I can't believe this. You're kidding, right?"

The publisher said nothing but gave Nick what might have been a sympathetic look. She walked back into the *Blade* building with Morton, leaving the reporter alone with his boss in the parking lot.

The C-Man instructed Nick to go home and file the report. "Take a break, think about the situation, and then write it up for me, okay? Morton and his banker friend are going to want your head on a platter. Give this some time to cool down, and we'll see what happens. I'll fight for you, but let's not do anything to make it worse."

Nick nodded. "But I'm working on what looks to be a great story. This ice-fishing death is really taking some turns, and now I'm suspended because an intern went out and got fried?" The reporter threw his notebook in the back seat of his car, more determined than ever to chase the story. "Well, a suspension—or a firing, for that matter—isn't going to stop me."

The managing editor encouraged Nick once again to give the issue time to blow over. He headed back to the *Blade* newsroom.

Nick grabbed a towel out of his trunk and wiped down the dashboard, seats, and console of the 'Bird. The suspension stung, but it did not hurt nearly as much as the sight inside his Firebird. He pulled out the floor mats gingerly and dumped them in the parking lot next to Morton Reynolds' driver's side door.

"Gosh, it would be awful if he tracked that into his car," he said to no one in particular. "And even worse if he carried it into his house."

The reporter finished cleaning his car, then called Dave to plan handling the story while he was on suspension. Carl Huffmann's funeral was an event he was looking forward to covering, Morton Reynolds or not.

Chapter 20

The day of Carl Huffmann's funeral, hundreds of his relatives, friends, neighbors, and associates turned up at the neighborhood-style funeral home in Owendale despite cold temperatures, well below freezing, and a bone-chilling wind. Visitors filled every seat and corner, sometimes bumping into one another as they moved about to talk and to pay their respects.

The funeral home was a small-community operation. The mortuary was run with great grace and professionalism by Phillip Plante and Edith Moore from inside a three-story home in a residential neighborhood. The couple had been together for years but had never married. In addition to the funeral chapel, the owners offered barbershop and beauty parlor services through a side entrance to the home. Model tombstones dotted the backyard. Customized grave markers could be purchased through the funeral home gift shop, located in the basement. The couple lived on the home's third level.

This morning the inside of the Plante-Moore Funeral Parlor looked like a greenhouse—plants and flowers lined every wall from top to bottom. Big bouquets of fresh flowers, decorated with ribbons and ornate condolence cards, came from all elements of the Thumb agricultural community, including the local farmers' cooperative, the Thumb National Bank—the largest ag lender in the region—multiple seed companies, a half-dozen fertilizer firms, local farm implement outlets, and agricultural techs from Michigan State University.

Local business and education leaders attended the ceremonies too, as did news reporters with the *Huron Daily Tribune* and the *Huron County View*. They sat with Nick Steele and Dave Balz of *The Bay*

City Blade. Though the news organizations were fierce competitors, they put their eye-scratching and hair-pulling proclivities aside for a couple hours in the name of decency and dignity. Each of their publications had carried news articles about the tragic events on Wild Fowl Bay, as well as obituaries for the late but no-so-great Mr. Huffmann.

Betty Huffmann, dressed in black from head to toe, including a long, thick, dark veil, greeted visitors while dabbing a small white handkerchief to her nose and eyes. Occasionally she would sob and wail or appear weak in the knees. Each time she did, Tom and Richard Huffmann rolled their eyes and high-fived each other.

The two brothers—the third brother, Bill, did not attend—tried to speak with every visitor. Many inquired about the boys' late mother, Joyce, who had passed more than a dozen years before. No members of her family attended the service. Too many hard feelings, too many bad memories for that branch of the family tree to participate. Even Bill had left a voice message for Richard to "send the old man on to hell, where he belongs, and just cut me a check when it's over."

The visitors were particularly keen to talk with Tom. They were eager to console the survivor and make sure he understood how lucky he was, but they also wanted to hear firsthand all the juicy details of the harrowing ordeal.

Tom had expected plenty of questions; he had spent the previous evening with his brother, rehearsing a general narrative that he could quickly recount to satisfy the masses. If they pressed for too many details and Tom felt uncomfortable, he would signal Richard to bail him out of the conversation by pulling on his own right earlobe. The two agreed this would only work if Richard stayed close to Tom and did not get dragged away by enthusiastic relatives or friends.

The tactic worked for a while, but the curiosity among folks in a small town who knew each other too well became overwhelming for Tom. Finally he feigned a bout of crippling grief, covered his eyes with one hand, and retreated to the men's room. He hid in the stalls until he heard organ music, which he figured signaled the start of the official service. Then he straightened his tie, pushed his hair back into place, and joined the others, eager to get the service behind him.

Carl had often railed against ministers who preached the Holy Word on Sundays but spent every other day of the week dipping into the collection plate or diddling the wives of church members. So it was no surprise to those in attendance that the only religious service would be a soft sermon by a local minister, nor that this preacher was not a representative from one of the four local Protestant congregations that Carl Huffmann had once been a member of but ultimately turned his back on and walked away.

The tribute, delivered by the Rev. Rodney Horney, lasted exactly seven minutes. When he finished, he asked members of the audience to step forward and share fond memories of the dearly departed.

No one did. Most at the service sat awkwardly, searching their memories for a touching tribute or a fitting story about Carl Huffmann to share. Tom and Richard, sitting next to each other with their heads bowed, smiled when it seemed no one would accept the Rev. Horney's invitation.

After several minutes an older gentleman stood and raised his hand. The reverend eagerly acknowledged Lenny, a retiree who was a frequent participant in discussions at the Old-Timers Table, an informal coffee klatch that met in Walt's Restaurant in downtown Caseville. In recent years Carl had become a regular at the table, which gathered most mornings. Sometimes he contributed anecdotes from his many years of living and farming in the area.

"I got a pretty good story to share about Carl from his school days," Lenny said. He cleared his throat twice and took a deep breath. "He told it more than once at the Old-Timers Table. We all told stories about when we were kids. Anyway, Carl's story went like this: 'When I was in eighth grade, everybody looked up to me—even the teachers. Of course, I was seventeen at the time.'"

The tale drew nervous laughter from the audience. One older gentleman called out, "That's Carl for you—he was a real potlicker!" The remark drew even more chuckles than Lenny's story.

Rev. Horney stepped back to the podium and asked if anyone else had a remembrance to share. Then three young ladies at the back of the room rose together. The tallest and largest of the three said she wanted to tell about their favorite "Christmas time with Daddy."

The remark drew gasps from the crowd. Tom and Richard almost snapped their necks turning to see the speakers.

Betty Huffmann headed off the threesome before their tale could be recounted. "Oh, no you don't." She faced the three women, flicked back her veil, and pointed a shaky finger at them. "We're not accepting any words from Carl's bastard children or his whore girlfriends. You can sit right back down or leave, but you are not being recognized or acknowledged today."

The woman speaking for the three sisters was tall and broad-shouldered and had the same sharp facial features as Carl. Her name was Carlina. She and her equally tall sisters, Carla and Carlotta, were from the Caro area, another small community in the Thumb.

Their mom, Gertrude, was the head cook at a German restaurant called the Speisesaal, of which Carl had been a silent partner. The three daughters worked for their mom, and together they made a good living for themselves.

Carl had visited the women and the restaurant often, claiming his trips to Caro were searches for farm equipment. The women had known Carl had another life and another family, but not much beyond that.

Now that Carlina had seized the spotlight, she was not going to be silenced easily. "We were closer to Daddy than any of you," she said. "And you're not going to shut us up. We will see you in court."

Gasps and throaty whispers spread across the audience like big Lake Huron rollers. Rev. Horney stepped back to the podium and tried to regain control of the rowdy service before it went right off the cliff. "Please, please, remember why we're here," he said. "Please respect the man who has passed, and this service."

Carlina was on a roll. "Cut the crap, Reverend. Everybody here knows Carl was a cantankerous son of a bitch, but they also know he was an SOB with a boatload of money. That's why so many are here. We all want to know what our cut of his dough is going to be."

"You're not getting a dime," Betty shrieked, trying to climb over the laps of the people seated next to her. "I just want to get my hands around your fat, sloppy neck."

Fat-shaming Carlina was not a wise decision on Betty's part. The words infuriated the younger woman, and clenching her fists so tightly her knuckles turned white, she moved toward Betty. "Bring it, you skinny bitch," Carlina said. "If you're going to take me on, you better bring dinner, because it's going to be an all-day job."

Carlina's sisters stood behind her, defiance written all over their faces.

By now most of the audience was standing too. A few tried to calm the women, calling for a return to civility and order. But it was too late. They charged at each other like gladiators in the ring. The two women were colliding forces who obviously had tangled before.

Through the arms of a man trying to restrain her, Betty grabbed a handful of Carlina's hair with one hand and tried to cold-cock her with the free fist. Her opponent swung her purse, a big leather number with a pair of long shoulder straps, at Betty. It knocked off her pillbox hat and heavy veil.

Rev. Horney banged on the podium with his fist. "Please, please, everyone. Take your seats. This is so unbecoming of you."

"Get bent, Reverend," Carlina said. "I'm getting my pound of flesh today, and nobody is going to deprive me of it."

After several minutes of wild melee, Deputy Jay-Bob Ratchett stepped in front of the open casket and removed his pistol from its holster. He raised the revolver in the air and shouted for the crowd to quiet.

"Now, don't make me use this weapon," he said. "I have one bullet in my holster belt, and I am authorized by the county sheriff to use it if I believe it is necessary to protect human life. And that means every one of you, except for Carl here, of course."

The sight of the revolver did the trick. Instantly those in attendance simmered down and then retook their seats, including the warring women. Rev. Horney smoothed out his combover, which was so mussed it resembled a tattered bird's nest. The breast pocket on his black suit coat had been torn and frayed in the confrontation, and his necktie was askew.

Katie tried to comfort her mom, refastening the pillbox hat and adjusting the veil, which was now shredded on one side. Betty's black dress had a dusty footprint on her right buttock, though no one dared brush it away.

Tom turned to Richard. "What the hell just happened, and who are those three women in the back? My god, what could possibly happen next?"

"I'm afraid to find out," Richard said, watching Betty sit back down. "But it sounds like we might have sisters—at least until the money is split up. We all knew the old man was a bastard, but the idea that he cheated on Mom, too, is sickening. A new low, even for him."

Rev. Horney, still shaken and wobbly, concluded the service, inviting all to participate in a final graveside tribute and then attend a luncheon put together by the Caseville Eagles Club, of which the old man had been a longstanding member. People filed out of the chapel in silence while the pallbearers assembled near Carl.

While the stunned folks exited the funeral home, Nick hustled to introduce himself to Carlina before she and her sisters could leave. He was relieved no one else had approached the three women as they walked to their car.

"Excuse me—I know this is a very difficult time for you," Nick said. He fumbled in his jacket pocket for a card to give the women. "I was wondering if I could talk with you for a few minutes."

The women stopped and faced him. At six two and 220 pounds, Nick was a fair-sized man, but Carl's daughters stood over him. Though they were obviously still upset by what had happened in the funeral home, they managed to smile at him as Nick finished identifying himself. Carlina offered her hand.

"We didn't come here to be quoted in the newspaper," she said. "We came here for our dad. We knew it would be hostile territory, but some things you do because you just have to."

"I respect that," Nick said. "But I wanted to say hello and express my condolences. I wondered if I could call you or visit you at another time."

"Sure, you can always find one of us at the Speisesaal in Caro," Carlina said. She introduced her sisters to Nick. They shook hands, and the reporter felt comfortable with them right away. "My mom's often there too," Carlina said. "She wanted to come today but was afraid it would get too emotional. Once again she was right."

Nick thanked them and jotted down the name of the restaurant, pausing to ask for help with the spelling.

"It's German for 'dining hall,'" Carla said. "You won't mistake it for another restaurant in the phone book, that's for sure."

Her remark prompted light laughter, which eased the tension of the moment. By now vehicles with black-and-white flags on their front fenders had lined up behind the hearse. The women said they had decided not to go to the cemetery because they did not want to be the source of any more drama. They shook hands again with Nick, and he raced to get the 'Bird in line.

Far toward the front, Tom and Richard rode to the cemetery in one of the funeral home's two long, black Lincoln Continentals, discussing their next steps. Tom said he wanted to speak with Betty as soon as the final prayers were recited at the grave. Richard urged him to wait because of what had played out at the funeral home.

"No, I just want to get this over with. The sooner the better," Tom said. "Betty has no use for me, and I really don't care to see her again. I'm going to ask her to move out immediately."

But Richard was in favor of letting them stay on at the farmhouse a bit longer. Tom didn't understand this sudden burst of generosity and Richard's compassion for Betty. He wondered whether Richard was trying to chum up with her or if they'd spoken privately without Tom's knowledge. If they were trying to make some kind of private side deal about the farm, it would change how Tom dealt with Richard in the future.

When they arrived at the cemetery, Tom noted that only a handful of cars had accompanied his dad to his final resting place. It did not take long for the dozen or so folks who'd parked alongside the tombstones to assemble at the grave. They stood close together, huddled against the biting wind.

Rev. Horney's final remarks and a solemn prayer were delivered in record time. Then Carl's casket was lowered into the ground while a few onlookers tossed small bouquets of flowers onto the lid as it fell out of view. When it was over and the groundskeepers moved into position with their shovels, Tom approached Betty to speak with her.

"Richard and I have been talking," he said, keeping his voice low. "We'd like you and your daughter to leave the farmhouse as soon as possible. We will take possession, as spelled out in the prenuptial agreement you signed when you married the old man."

Betty simply regarded Tom with a sour expression. After a minute or two she reached into her small black purse and pulled out two sheets of paper. "I knew you would pull this," she said, and thrust the paperwork at Tom. "You are as predictable as a sunset. You're as emotional as a teenage girl too, and I've been able to read you like a book ever since I moved into the farmhouse."

Betty waved the papers in front of Tom's face, declaring in a loud voice, "Here is the letter of revocation of our prenuptial agreement, signed by Carl and me and duly notarized, I might add. My daughter and I are not going anywhere. The farm is mine. You can swing by and pick up your junk this weekend. I'm having it all moved out to the barn tomorrow."

Richard said nothing. Tom stammered, then protested. "What? I don't believe it," he said. "The old man must have lost his mind. When was that signed? This won't stand up in court. This is our family legacy."

"Two months ago," she said, handing the letter to Tom. "Here's a copy for you and your records. Here's the updated will. Carl left you and your brothers $25,000 each. You'll get that when the estate is settled." Betty stepped back as if she expected a violent reaction. "And don't forget to pick up your trash, or I'll send it all to Goodwill."

Tom read the letter of revocation and the will, his anger rising. He wadded the papers into small balls and threw them into the grave. They bounced on top of the casket and rolled to one side.

Tom followed the letter, going feet first into the grave and landing on the casket with both feet. "No, no, no, no. I do not believe it!" He jumped up and down on the casket like a youngster on a trampoline. "You bastard. You dirty, rotten SOB."

Richard dropped to one knee next to the grave and let his head settle in the palms of his hands. Betty walked away from the gravesite and the two outraged young men, a crisp, sly smile on her face.

Nick Steele snapped off a half-dozen or so photos with his cell phone. The other two news reporters had not followed the hearse to the gravesite, which meant Nick alone had some excellent photos to go with an article detailing the drama that had engulfed Carl Huffmann's funeral. All was not well in this prominent farm family, and it was about to spill out for full public consumption in the pages of *The Bay City Blade.*

Chapter 21

As a rooster crowed to welcome dawn to the Huffmann farm on Thursday morning, Betty and Katie hustled about the house, getting ready for the long list of visitors who had been summoned to the homestead.

Betty had plans, big plans for the farm. The old-fashioned country kitchen, with its rough, handmade pine cabinets and wood plank floor, would soon be a thing of the past. New cupboards, countertops, appliances, and Italian marble flooring were at the top of her list. The home's three bathrooms would be updated next, including the expansion of one into a master bath with a walk-in shower and a massive jet tub for Betty. She had decided to combine the three upstairs bedrooms for Katie, turning the space into a small apartment with its own private kitchen and bath and a separate entrance.

By ten o'clock, local contractors would begin arriving to map out plans for the renovations. But before that, Betty was expecting another visitor. She looked out the kitchen window and watched a shiny black Lincoln Navigator amble up the driveway.

The sales manager at Ordus Ford in Bad Axe had brought it out to Betty to test drive for a few days. If she liked it, Betty would write him a check for $62,650. "I'm done driving farm trucks," she'd told the manager on the phone. "Bring me the nicest SUV you got—I want all the bells and whistles—and make sure it's shiny."

While Betty marveled at the new Lincoln parked in her drive, another vehicle approached the house. Two of Katie's high school friends were going to make two hundred dollars apiece for a day of hauling junk from the house to the barn. Most of the items belonged to Tom, but his brothers still had a considerable amount of stuff in the old farmhouse, even though they had not lived there in years. Betty wanted it all out before the end of the day. Carl's boys could recover it from the pigsty, she decided—if they wanted it.

The two young guys followed Katie into the house, where she introduced them to the hundreds of items that had to be moved. Betty, meanwhile, could hardly wait to have some fun with her new toy. She climbed into the driver's seat of the Lincoln and fired up its powerful engine.

When the younger threesome arrived on the second level of the house to begin the move, they looked out the window just in time to see Betty trying out her new Lincoln in an empty hayfield. She was making figure eights and fishtailing all over the place, playing like a pup with a new squeaky toy.

Just as she ran the SUV to the end of the field and slid sideways the last hundred feet, another vehicle entered the driveway. Betty turned back to the house and met Deputy Ratchett as he pulled up near the garage. He did not jump out of the cruiser immediately, which told her he wanted her to come to him so they could talk privately.

"Hi, Ace. Wondered if you'd be by today," she said from the black leather bucket seat of the Navigator. A Dwight Yoakam country tune boomed from the sparkling SUV's stereo system.

Jay-Bob seemed impressed with the vehicle despite the thousands of blades of grass stuck to its lower back end. "Girl, you did not waste a minute getting a new ride. Who are all the guys moving in and out of your house?"

Betty shut off the SUV and slid out of the driver's seat. She was wearing designer blue jeans, a tight red sweater, and a dark-brown corduroy jacket. Betty knew she looked hot and did not mind flaunting her new appearance in front of Jay-Bob.

"Doing a little renovation," she said, moving closer to Jay-Bob without making physical contact. "Carl was just too damn cheap to spend any money on the place or on me. We're both way overdue for some sprucing up."

Betty told the deputy that she also planned on a visit from the wind turbine developers. Neighbors had already signed up to be part of the next mega wind farm in the Thumb, and the new queen of the Huffmann homestead wanted to hear what they had to say—and peek inside their deep pockets. Carl's resistance to joining the wind energy movement had become a great source of frustration and tension between Tom and his dad. Betty had stayed out of the battle, preferring to let them bang away at each other while she smiled and nodded. Now that she was in control of the farm, she planned to rake in all the money she could, and fast.

Jay-Bob reached back into his cruiser and handed Betty a legal document. It was a warrant allowing the deputy to search the property—specifically, Tom Huffmann's belongings—for anything that might be related to the death of Carl Huffmann. She took her time reading it from top to bottom, then folded the paper and tossed it into the Lincoln.

"I'll get you the rest of Tom's paperwork—the diaries, journals, and whatnot—but you'll have to hustle to go through his room," she said, brushing her long dark hair back from her face. "Katie just took two of her friends upstairs so they can haul his crap out of the house. Going to get the other brothers' stuff out of there too."

Betty walked Jay-Bob into the house and watched him disappear up the stairway to the second floor. The moment the deputy was out of view, she ran to the pantry cupboard, where she had stored Tom's voluminous writings. She set them on the kitchen table, then went after Jay-Bob—to make sure he wasn't snooping around the house where he wasn't supposed to be.

She found him in Tom's bedroom, thumbing through a high school yearbook.

"Who is Tim Fisher?" he asked.

"Just an old buddy." She settled into a chair near a window that overlooked a harvested cornfield, then kicked her feet up on a footstool and leaned back. It seemed the whole world was spinning in her direction these days. "Haven't seen him around in a while."

"Could be a witness," Jay-Bob said. "He wrote a note in the yearbook—says he'll help Tom take care of his old man. 'Just let me know when,' he wrote. Then he sketched a skull and crossbones under his name. I'll bet the prosecutor will want to talk with him."

Betty smoothed out the wrinkles in her fancy new jeans and watched the deputy flip through multiple pages.

"You know, I'm getting a little nervous about this," she said. "I don't think you should come out here anymore. In fact, I don't think we should have any contact at all for the next year."

"What? That's not what we talked about," Jay-Bob said. "I love you, Sweet Cheeks. You know that. How are you going to get along without me for that long? I will be one horny SOB by then."

Betty forced a laugh, then reached over and patted Jay-Bob on the knee. "There, there. You'll be okay, and if you're not, you'll just have to go back to dating your right hand."

"Oh, you are so nasty," the deputy said. "I should pull you right over here on this bed and make you pay for your insolence."

Betty laughed again and jumped to her feet before Jay-Bob could make a move. She motioned for the deputy to follow her back to the kitchen, where she had stacked Tom's writings. "Here you go. Should make some fine reading," she said.

Jay-Bob took the notebooks. Betty opened the door leading to the back porch, hoping the deputy would get the hint that it was time for him to go.

"Betty, I can't wait a year to see you," he said, not moving toward the open door. With his droopy eyes and expressionless face, he looked like a hound dog that had just lost its master.

"Too dangerous," she said. "Strangers are in the house right now. Someone might see or hear us. No more contact until this blows over."

"But Sweet Cheeks, please—"

"If we find any more stuff of Tom's that will help you, I will have Katie contact you. I'll get in touch when I think it's safe. And quit calling me that."

Jay-Bob walked out of the kitchen, notebooks and yearbook in tow, without saying a word.

Betty closed the door before he was off the porch. She watched him walk to his cruiser, then called out to Katie, who was still upstairs directing the movers. When her daughter came downstairs, Betty pulled her into the pantry and closed the door.

"I got a horrible feeling that Jay-Bob could become a problem," she said, her voice barely above a whisper. "What an ass. Put your thinking cap on. We have to figure another plan with him."

Katie smiled at her mother. "There's always an accident waiting to happen," she said. "We just have to find it."

Chapter 22

The law offices of Robert L. Skinner were empty Thursday morning when Tom and Richard entered from the bustling street just off Van Dyke Road near downtown Bad Axe. Tom had called the attorney Wednesday night after he and his brother got home from the funeral.

They took seats in the small entryway of the office, which looked as though it had been decorated by a blind man with a Salvation Army budget. No receptionist was on duty. The walls were covered with mobile-home paneling. The indoor/outdoor carpeting had not been introduced to a steam cleaner in years, and the chairs were wood frame with Styrofoam cushions and vinyl covering that had been patched up with duct tape.

Tom checked the time on his cell. Bob Skinner, whom Richard knew from their days in high school, would not be back from court until ten o'clock. The brothers had time to kill, and neither was talkative. They played games on their cell phones, pausing occasionally to note that a handful of minutes had passed.

While they waited, another young man—recently graduated from high school, Tom guessed—entered the office. He was tall and lanky, with a baseball cap perched backward on his head. The kid wore faded work jeans, a stained hooded sweatshirt, and high lace-up boots. The aroma that followed the guy into the waiting area told Tom the stains came from toil in a barnyard. A pair of tattered leather gloves stuck out of the top of his rear pants pocket.

Tom did not know the man's name, but something about him looked familiar. He couldn't put a finger on it, and that bothered him. Something about his appearance ate at the younger Huffmann.

The young guy made directly for the closed door leading to Skinner's lair and banged on the door with the side of his balled-up fist. No response. After a few moments he banged the door again.

"Save your energy—nobody is here yet," Tom said, looking away from the younger guy and staring out the only window in the entryway. The window was filthy, but it didn't block the bright sunshine that flooded the room, warming it enough for the occupants to want to ditch their winter jackets. "We gotta see him too. He's supposedly over at the courthouse. Should be back soon."

"Figures. Damn lawyers, anyway," the young guy said. He paced the room, checking his cell for the time every couple of minutes. "My brother got another drunk driving, and he's sitting over there in the county jail. We had a wild weekend fishing and drinking. Now I'm here to bail him out, and then we both got to get to work, or we won't have shit to give the attorney."

Tom did not reply. Richard didn't look up from his game. They both knew lots of young guys with that same sad tale to tell.

At 10:28 a.m. the office door finally swung open. Bob Skinner didn't bother to say hello, and he didn't bother to apologize for being late. He simply told the young guy to post bail and go pick up his brother. "I think he's still drunk. Smells like it, and he's staggering when he walks."

The kid thanked Bob and asked him how much it was going to cost. The attorney said the second drunk driving would cost more than the first. He told him to keep his brother out of the bars and start saving his money.

When the young guy left, the attorney motioned for Richard and Tom to come into the office.

"So you got squeezed out of your inheritance, huh?" Bob said, more as a statement of fact than a question.

"Yeah, and we want to know what we can do now," Richard said.

He seemed agitated; Tom noticed he did not take a seat. "The old man had a ton of money tied up in that farm," Richard said, slamming his open palm onto the desk. The bang startled the attorney, who finally looked interested. "The land and equipment are worth millions of bucks."

Tom nodded in agreement. He said he knew that Carl and Betty had signed a prenuptial agreement because they had agreed property "should always—and forever—remain in the hands of Huffmanns," or so his dad had said. Neither Tom nor Richard had had any idea that the prenuptial had been revoked. The will, allotting a meager $25,000 to each Huffmann son, had surprised him as well.

"I didn't even know a prenup could be revoked," Tom said. "And the will was revised without our knowledge. So now what? Are we screwed?"

"Pretty much," Bob said. "We can sue and challenge it, but Michigan law is pretty clear when it comes to marriage. If there's a split between the couple, the wife gets at least half. If he dies, she gets it all."

"But what about us?" Tom and Richard said at the same time. "What's gotta happen here?"

"Does Betty have to disappear?" Tom said.

"Is her death the only way we get back into the game?" Richard asked. He moved to the side of the attorney's desk and sat down.

"I'm going to pretend I didn't hear that," Bob said. "Let me get into the paperwork and see what I can find out. Did you get copies of the prenup and the revocation? The will?"

Richard glanced at Tom, who told the attorney that their copies were in the vault with their old man—the result of a fit of anger. The brothers looked like they'd just eaten something that had spoiled days ago.

Skinner sighed. He asked the brothers if they had noticed any signs that their dad was losing his faculties. Could relatives, friends, or neighbors attest to a decline in Carl's mental state? he asked.

Richard shrugged, saying he'd had almost no contact with Carl over the past five years. Tom said his old man had been the same cranky bastard he'd been for the last twenty-five years. "So what should we do next?" he asked.

"Nothing—let me get into it," Bob said. "I'll figure out a game plan, and we'll go from there. And don't go spending that twenty-five grand before you get it."

He told the brothers they had the right to retrieve their personal possessions from the farm, but they should be cautious. "Only go there by invitation," he said. "And make sure people are around when you are on the property or removing your things. You want witnesses. Use your cell phones to record what happens while you are there."

The brothers left the law office disheartened. They had hoped for legal relief or something approaching optimism from the attorney, but all they could see now was a long court battle with an uncertain result. They decided to get out of the Thumb.

Chapter 23

Nick flipped through Thursday's *Bay City Blade* while he worked at his dining room table. His suspension from the paper meant he could not use the *Blade* newsroom, but it didn't mean he had to quit developing his story. He had labored late into the night and filed his piece first thing that morning. The C-Man had emailed him a note of thanks for more great work.

The managing editor also said that Gordon was doing better. Apparently his dad had taken him to McLaren Bay Region in Bay City, where the intern's stomach was pumped after he confessed to nurses that he had taken a few pills, snorted some white stuff, smoked a short, flat pipe, and washed it all down with screwdrivers.

"That's why the mess in the 'Bird was orange," Nick said aloud, shaking his head. The reporter had spent three hours cleaning the inside of his prized vehicle.

Nick's boss also mentioned that Gordon's work on Wild Fowl Bay was a bust. The kid had only talked to one ice fisherman, the C-Man wrote, and focused on the fact that the guy was a collector of guns and knives, ignoring or forgetting his assignment. He'd spent the rest of his time on the ice partying with the collector until they moved to the Bluewater Inn.

Nick saved the note in his protected email file. He felt vindicated but also sorry for Gordon, who had missed an opportunity to display his reporting and writing skills—very important for interns. But the missed opportunity gave Nick an idea. He called the young reporter who had not gotten the internship and asked if he was interested in working on a freelance story. The answer was, predictably, yes. Nick invited the young scribe to his apartment Friday afternoon, where he planned to outline the project, giving the kid the same rundown he'd given Gordon.

Nick opened the newspaper so the whole front page lay in front of him. His ice-fishing story and photos, which dominated the front page of *The Blade*, were the talk of the town and the Thumb. The main photo showed Tom Huffmann jumping up and down on his father's casket, with his brother on one knee beside the grave and his stepmother walking away with a smile on her face like Cruella DeVil. The shot had prompted heated debate in the newsroom before it was published, Clapper had told Nick.

Some of the newsroom editors and reporters had thought the photo was insensitive and violated the family's privacy. Others found it completely appropriate and extraordinarily telling, especially since Nick had been invited to attend the funeral services and authorized to take photos. This was a family in complete distress, and the photo displayed its dysfunction.

The managing editor had finally settled the discussion, deciding to run the photograph with Nick's report, on the front page above the fold. Soon after the paper hit the streets, telephone calls piled up in the newsroom. Some readers were outraged by the photo, saying that graveside rites were sacred and should not be open to public scrutiny. Newsroom clerks fielded calls all afternoon.

To Nick, the Huffmann family had clearly come unhinged. His instincts told him there was much more going on with the family than the tragic accident that had claimed the life of the patriarch.

And he could not shake the thought of the cement-filled pipe and what role it had played in the saga. The wrench with skin and hair on it was bothering him too. He wondered if that could have been planted evidence, but he couldn't think by whom, and for what purpose.

Nick had not mentioned the wrench and human tissue in his story because it was merely unconfirmed gossip between county employees, something he'd picked up at the coffee shop. If it turned out to be a weapon that was used in Carl's demise, that would cast a whole new light on the family saga.

To get that crucial piece of information confirmed, Nick had placed a call to the Fairview fire chief that morning, hoping the man who had overseen the rescue and recovery effort might be willing to enlighten him.

Nick moved to his living room with the paper tucked under his arm. He used his free hand to sweep the dozen empty beer cans off the coffee table, splashing warm, stale-smelling liquid onto the carpet. Fortunately a whistle brought Jenni to come take care of the spills, which she happily did.

Earlier the reporter had whipped up a batch of bacon and eggs for breakfast. The lingering aroma made Jenni lick her chops now. Nick patted the lovable pooch on the head. Jenni burped. It smelled like beer, which meant it was time for her to go home. He opened the door a crack, and she shot out.

Working from home had its benefits. The privacy allowed Nick to lounge around his apartment in his T-shirt and underwear. The only guy who'd ever gotten away with that in the newsroom was a copy editor called Crazy Louie, now deceased. He'd been forced to wear his jacket wrapped around his waist when women or visitors came into the newsroom.

While Nick waited for the chief, a different call brought his cell to life. His girlfriend, Tanya, was on the line, and Nick had not talked with her in more time than he liked.

Their relationship might best be described as complex but odd. The two had found great love for each other, but they were constantly pulled apart by their life passions. Nick, Tanya had discovered, was married to his work as a journalist. And Tanya, Nick knew, was a devoted and dedicated educator. They could never quite seem to get on the same page. Their story had become a book with never-concluding chapters.

Even so, the relationship had been good for them both. Nick had worked hard at stabilizing the way he lived. He no longer saw the need for binge drinking, the once destructive force in his life. Tanya, he thought, saw Nick as a kind of daddy figure; he was twelve years her senior and had helped her get through the loss of her father, which had had a devastating effect on her family.

Though the couple experienced dramatic ups and downs like most others, they remained committed and would not allow either one to give up on the other.

The two had planned a long vacation together in Key West the previous fall, hoping the chance for time together without the usual distractions would take their relationship to a higher level. They would spend the days holding hands and enjoying long walks and fabulous sunsets while creating bonds that would last a lifetime. They also both intended to consummate their relationship, which would seal the deal, so to speak.

But alas, none of that had happened. Tanya's mother, Isabella, had been diagnosed with breast cancer, and the news of her illness had derailed their plans. Tanya was consumed by her work at UM and with trying to help her mother combat the deadly disease. The result was less time with Nick, who could not protest the idea that he would have to take a back seat in the competition for Tanya's time and attention.

These days Nick valued any time they could get. He took her phone call with great anticipation. "Hey, sweetheart, what's happening?"

"I'm still in Ann Arbor, and I can't seem to get out of here," she said. "I saw your story and photo online in the *Detroit Free Press* this morning, so I just had to call."

"I'm glad you did," he said, relaxing back into the sofa. The sound of her voice gave Nick great joy. He missed her. "I would have called you this afternoon if I hadn't heard from you. Got a really good story going here, and I wanted to bounce some ideas off you."

Tanya said she had been busy with final exams at the University of Michigan. She was working on getting a new teaching certificate— another advanced degree to help reach children with learning disabilities. Her professors, she said, were merciless.

"Besides, you've always got Dave up there to use as a sounding board," she told him, laughing. "You two make a great team—if you can keep from getting fired again."

"Ah, at the moment I'm suspended from *The Blade*," Nick said, his voice trailing off. He hated telling her that he was in trouble once more. "It's a long story—I'll tell you about it when I see you. Now, are you coming home, or am I going to have to make a run to Ann Arbor myself?"

Tanya said she hoped to be home over the weekend but could not count on it because of the demands of her studies. She was shooting for an arrival Saturday morning.

Nick's cell phone indicated he had another call: the fire chief.

"Gotta get this—talk to you later, baby," Nick said, clicking Tanya off before she could say good-bye. He suspected he was going to pay for cutting her off like that, but he had no choice. If the reporter was lucky, he might get the chief to volunteer information about a weapon being found.

The sound of the fire chief's voice made Nick sit up straight on the edge of his couch. He decided to dive right in. "Ben, I interviewed the ME, who said the cut on the drowning victim's forehead was caused by a blow to the head," Nick told the chief. "The sheriff's department would not confirm that, but I heard from some county employees that a weapon was found."

Nick allowed a long pause to linger for what seemed like an eternity. Then the chief exhaled slowly. "Aw, shit."

More silence. Nick baited his hook. "Chief, did you find a weapon out on the ice near where Mr. Huffmann drowned?"

Again silence, and then finally a response. "Ah, yeah, well, I didn't find it, but my guys kinda did."

"What was it, and how did they know it was a weapon?"

"They found an adjustable wrench—a crescent wrench—on an ice floe out by where the Huffmanns went into the lake," the chief said. "Now, you can't quote me on this. It's got to come from the sheriff or the prosecutor."

"Okay, but what made you think it was used as a weapon?" Nick used the softest voice he could muster while still remaining audible; he did not want to intimidate the chief or scare him off the interview.

"Some skin and hair were wedged into the knurl," the chief said, his voice filled with resignation. It was clear he wanted the truth to become public, but he was fearful the unauthorized release of information would come back to haunt him.

"The what?"

"Skin and hair in the knurl, or the worm," he said.

Nick let that settle in for a moment. "So is it being tested?"

"Yup, they put a rush on it. Could get results anytime now," the chief said. He paused, like he wanted the reporter to pay close attention to what he was about to say. "Nick, you've got to promise me one thing. You didn't get this info from me. Remember that. If I hear my name attached to that report, or you, I will deny, deny, deny until I die."

"No worry," Nick said. He tried to contain his excitement at the confirmation of the wrench and human tissue. "The prosecutor and the sheriff hate each other. I'll just play one off the other and leverage it out of one or both of them. Thanks, chief!"

Before they hung up, the reporter asked for one clarification: he wanted a definition for the knurl and worm.

"Easy," the chief said. "It's the mechanism that adjusts the jaw and size of the wrench. Some people call it a worm because that's what it looks like."

Nick wondered if the worm had turned on this case.

Chapter 24

Since Nick could not go into work because of his suspension, he decided to meet Dave at O'Hare's Pub while he waited for the Huron County prosecutor to return his call—hopefully that afternoon.

Being suspended did have its advantages, Nick thought to himself again as he walked down Midland Street toward the noted saloon on Bay City's West Side. He figured it was time to touch base with the Huron County sheriff, who he knew would not offer any information at all about the possible new evidence. Even so, he had to lay the question on the sheriff.

"Can't comment on that," the sheriff said immediately. "We are continuing to gather information about the tragic death on Wild Fowl Bay."

The lawman tried to shut the door on the telephone interview, but Nick stuck his foot in the way. He was ready to handle a brush-off.

"But sheriff, Huron County employees are openly talking about you finding a wrench with skin and hair on it," Nick said, hoping to catch the sheriff off guard by bombing him with information that he did not have. "Are you saying that there's nothing to this? That what's being commented on publicly is not true?"

Nick could hear the sheriff fumbling with the phone and grunting quietly. "Ah, again, I can't comment on the weapon or what was attached to it."

"Sheriff, okay, so it's true. The wrench had skin and hair stuck in its knurl?"

"Its what?"

"The knurl. That's the thing that adjusts the crescent wrench," Nick said.

"No shit. Is that what they call that thing? Never heard it before."

"Yes," Nick said. "It's called a knurl, and employees all across Huron County are talking about it. Can you confirm?"

"Well, hell no, I can't confirm. I have no idea what the parts of a crescent wrench are called."

The sheriff's response delighted Nick so much that he almost soiled himself. "No, I've been told by very reliable county employees that you found a crescent wrench with human tissue in it at the scene of the drowning on Wild Fowl Bay," Nick said. "Is that correct?"

"I can't control what county employees are saying," the sheriff said. "We don't know that it's human tissue. It's all been sent to the crime lab for analysis."

"Got it! Thanks, sheriff!" Nick clicked off his cell before the sheriff could retract what he'd said. Now Nick could go to the prosecutor and ask him to confirm that possible new evidence in the case had been sent to the crime lab.

When Nick entered the bar, he spotted Dave sitting in his usual spot at a table at the back of the bar. As the reporter walked underneath the upside-down Christmas tree attached to the ceiling of O'Hare's, he blew it a kiss. An Irish friend had told him that the gesture would always bring him good luck.

"Are you still throwing kisses at that tree?" Dave called out. "That legend is crap. How much luck have you had recently? You got suspended from *The Blade* again, and you're probably two steps ahead of getting the final boot out of the place."

The two friends laughed and high-fived each other. A bottle of beer, dripping with condensation, stood tall on the table in front of Nick's chair. He grabbed it by its neck and took a long, hard pull. Dave asked for an update. He'd read every word of his pal's piece in that day's paper, but he wanted the great stuff that hadn't made print.

Nick became animated, showing Dave how Tom Huffmann had jumped up and down on the casket. He also described the new evidence and the information he was gathering and getting confirmed.

Before long Sassy Sally, the longtime bartender, swung by their table. She asked what was causing all the commotion.

Nick started to tell her but was distracted by the entrance of two men through the back door of O'Hare's. He stopped talking mid-sentence and stared. Naturally, Dave and Sally followed his gaze to the passageway.

Richard and Tom Huffmann stood several feet from the three, looking for a place to sit down. Sally told the guys to pull up a chair anywhere, and she would be right with them.

The Huffmanns sat down two tables away from Nick and Dave. They talked quietly but stopped to place a drink order with the Sassy One. Nick leaned in close to Dave and explained who had just arrived at the bar.

The reporter wanted to introduce himself, but he was having trouble getting rid of the image of Tom dancing on his dad's casket. He wondered if Tom would remember seeing him at the services. He also wondered if the brothers had seen that day's front page—at least, he hoped they had not.

"Hi, I'm Nick Steele, a reporter with *The Bay City Blade*," he said, extending his hand. They shook. "First off, I want to extend my condolences to you and your family. I was going to say something to you yesterday during services, but you were continually surrounded by friends."

"Oh yeah, I do remember seeing you in Owendale yesterday," Tom said. Richard sat expressionless, sipping the draft that Sally had just dropped at the table. Bob Seger's "Like A Rock" blared from a jukebox at the other end of the bar, far enough away for the men to talk without shouting at each other.

Nick introduced himself to Richard, who he thought was hesitant to talk. He also introduced Dave to both brothers.

While they exchanged small talk, Sally brought two wooden tokens to the table and placed one in front of each of the Huffmanns. Tom asked the bartender what the tokens represented.

"A free drink," she said, motioning to two guys sitting at the pub's long oak bar. The men were grinning and giving the brothers a thumbs-up. "They said you deserved a beer because you've got a lot of guts."

The brothers looked at each other without speaking. Nick guessed that they had not seen that day's paper with their photo on the front page, but that the guys at the bar had and were expressing their approval. The reporter wasn't quite sure what to do. He had three options: not say anything to the brothers, finish their beers, and leave; fill the brothers in on what was in the paper; or just play dumb and wait to see what happened.

Nick picked option three. He and Dave were well-versed in playing dumb and hoping for the best—it often worked well for them when they were in hot water in the newsroom. But then again, sometimes not so much.

Within a few minutes Sassy Sally returned to the brothers' table with two more tokens in hand. This time the free booze came from a table full of guys who were sitting underneath the upside-down Christmas tree. Like the guys at the bar, they grinned and gave the brothers a thumbs-up.

"Are they doing that because we're from the Thumb?" Richard asked. "How the hell would they know that, anyway?"

Before Tom could respond, one of the men from the table

approached them. He was short and wide, dressed in jeans, a Detroit Red Wings sweatshirt, and a Lions knit beanie. Long brown hair flowed out from beneath the cap. The two or three days' worth of spotty whiskers on his face matched the color of his hair.

"Hey, guys, don't want to bust in on you, but I just had to say how much I admire you," Brown Whiskers said, smiling enough to reveal several missing teeth, both upper and lower. "Funerals are always tough, but for you to jump up and down on your dad's casket right there at the grave—wow, that was cool! Wish I would have had the nerve to do that when they buried my old man."

Nick decided he should visit the men's room, and Dave suddenly recognized an old friend at the other end of the bar whom he had an urge to visit. They scattered like mosquitos fleeing the flickering tongues of bullfrogs.

Brown Whiskers explained the photo on the front page of *The Blade*, and Nick's lengthy article about the funeral and the tragic death on Wild Fowl Bay.

"Don't tell me you didn't see it," he said, waving at one of his buddies at the table across the room. "Hey, Rex," he hollered at his friend, "you still got today's paper out in your truck? Go get it for these guys to see."

Tom looked for Nick and Dave, but the only signs of the men were empty jackets slung over their chairs and half-filled bottles of beer on the table.

While he waited for the reporters to return, the guys continued talking about their fathers and the poor relationships they had. Tom only half listened. Richard, too, remained distracted, sipping his beer.

When Nick returned from the restroom, the first thing he spotted was the Huffmann brothers reading *The Blade* at their table, surrounded by the guys who had just bought them beers. He looked for Dave, fearing that he might need more support than Sassy Sally could supply. Nick did not say anything; he simply stood at his table, sipped what was left of his beer, and waited for a possible storm to come his way.

Dave returned just as the brothers turned to an inside page to continue reading the remainder of the article. More photos, though not nearly as juicy as the one up front, accompanied the jump.

Within a few minutes, the brothers finished reading *The Blade*. Tom looked up and made laser eye contact with Nick.

"Nice article, but I'm surprised you used photos from the funeral," he said, folding the newspaper and handing it back to Rex. "Isn't that some kind of invasion of privacy or something?"

"Betty invited us, as well as the other media present," Nick said. "I asked for permission to take photographs, and she authorized it in writing. In fact, she suggested that I make sure I stayed until the end of the service—so glad I did. She said we could feel free to publish any photos we took."

"She wanted you to stay until the end?" Tom asked. "She probably figured I'd go nuclear."

"That bitch," Richard said, joining in the conversation. "Stepmothers are among the most evil people on earth."

"You got that right," Brown Whiskers said. "Not everybody's home life is like you see on *The Brady Bunch*. Every time I saw my stepmom, I looked to see where she'd parked her broom."

The guys laughed, easing the tension of the moment. The men who had gathered around the brothers' table high-fived each other and returned to their brews.

Nick motioned to Sassy Sally, who had stood nearby in case of trouble, to bring everyone a round of drinks. "And put it on Dave's tab—I'm not getting paid this week," he said.

As a third token was placed in front of the brothers, Nick asked if he could talk with them for a few minutes about their dad's passing. The reporter was emboldened by the brothers' reaction to the article and photos in *The Blade*. He had the feeling that the time might be perfect to engage them.

Tom shrugged. "We got a lot of drinking to do. We can listen while we do it."

Nick pulled a notebook out of his rear hip pocket and a pen from his jacket. He decided to plunge in with his toughest questions while they were friendly and talkative.

"So," he said. "Are you shocked that the cops think they've found a weapon in connection with your dad's death?"

"What weapon?" the brothers said together.

They both stood up from their chairs, but Tom took the lead. "What are you talking about? What weapon?"

Nick explained how he had learned from reliable sources that a wrench had been found with human tissue on it. He also told the brothers what the county medical examiner had said about the cut on Carl Huffmann's forehead—but that the doc was certain their dad had died from drowning. "The blow to his head may have dazed him or even knocked him out," Nick said, "but it did not kill him."

Tom said a sheriff's deputy had told him while he was in the hospital that a cut or gash had been discovered on his old man's head.

"But the last time I saw my dad, he was very much alive, and there were no cuts on his head that I observed," he said. "Of course it was dark and really nasty out there—and we were both trying to survive. Maybe he had a cut on his head and I didn't see it. He didn't complain about it, that's for sure."

Nick jotted notes as quickly as he could. "What was the last thing your dad said to you?"

"He told me to follow the Christmas tree lights, and I did. That's how I ended up at that cottage on Sand Point. Seems to me that you were there too."

Nick could see that Tom had tensed up and was getting irritated, but he had one more important question to ask him.

"Now, don't get pissed at me, but I have to ask you this question," Nick said. "Did you kill your father, or did you have anything to do with his death?"

"Absolutely not," Tom said. "He was alive and kicking the last time I saw him."

Nick reached over to his table and grabbed his beer. He downed the contents in three gulps, liquid leaking from the corners of his mouth and dripping down his chin.

"Excuse me, I've got a heck of a story to write," he said. "Can I get your cell number so I can call you? I'm pretty sure our paths will cross again."

Richard said they might be calling Nick or Dave in an hour or so—for a ride home. Each brother now had eight tokens stacked up on the table.

Chapter 25

Dave Balz ambled into the Shear Crazy Salon in downtown Pigeon on Saturday morning and approached the empty front counter. The studio bustled with activity. All four chairs in the cutting area were filled with women, who chatted with the stylists attending them.

The reporter surveyed the salon. Four hair dryers on cushioned lounge chairs lined the wall behind the cutting area. One corner of the neat and tidy studio was tucked behind a half privacy wall, where a nail technician was busy with a customer. A hallway toward the back of the building led to a tanning area on one side and a massage room on another. A bouquet of fresh-cut flowers graced each of the salon's four corners. A large potted peace lily stood at the edge of the front counter.

Dave had decided to stop by the salon on an information-gathering mission while Nick visited Tanya in Ann Arbor for the weekend. Shear Crazy was the only fully operational salon in the small farming village, and mostly women flocked to it. The guys tended to use the town's only barbershop, Ron's, which had a twirling, lit candy-striped sign out front. No women frequented the men's shop, and only a handful of brave guys ventured into the women's salon.

But Dave Balz was not an everyday kind of guy, and he really didn't care what people thought about him or what he did. He needed information about Betty Huffmann, and he figured Shear Crazy was the best place in town for a stranger to pick up some juicy tidbits.

Plus, Dave might best have been described as rough around the edges. It was time for him to clean up a bit. The activity in Shear Crazy confirmed for him that he'd made a good decision.

After a few minutes one of the hair stylists excused herself from her customer and walked to the counter to look Dave up and down. Her scowl told the reporter she was not impressed. Dave, already short and stocky, wore baggy blue jeans with a tan canvas jacket and a red flannel shirt, unbuttoned enough to reveal bushy sandy chest hair. But Dave smiled at the stylist and shook his untamed mop at her.

"I need the works," he said, pushing back his unruly brown hair, now heavily speckled with gray. Paying cash for a haircut was not something he was accustomed to. When his locks got out of control, he usually solved the problem by taking scissors and lopping off the troublesome areas.

"No kidding," the stylist said. Her nametag declared she was Tammy. Her spiked purple hair and nose ring said she was trying to stay young, though Dave guessed her age to be early thirties. Tammy wore an oversized fluorescent-green sweatshirt with the words "Bite Me" on the front and black leggings that were two sizes too small, revealing more of her full figure than the laws of decency would normally allow. Dave liked what he saw.

"Where do you want to start, big guy?" she said.

"My name is Dave. Haven't had a professional cut in a while," he said, grinning. He slipped off his jacket and leaned over the counter, placing the top of his head right in front of her face.

"No kidding," Tammy said again, peering into the thick, curly mop. She stuck her fingers in and tried to fluff it up. When she did, a sliver of wood popped out, startling her. "What the hell? You got a toothpick in there."

"I wondered what happened to that," Dave said, shaking his head slowly. "Put it behind my ear a couple days ago, then it just kinda disappeared."

Tammy pulled her hand back and said nothing could happen

until he'd had a thorough shampoo. "Then what do you want me to do with it?"

"You're the expert—fix it. I don't own a hair dryer, and I don't spend a lot of time fussin' in front of the mirror in the morning. Whatever you do, it's gotta be low-maintenance."

Tammy nodded and smiled. She said she would try to wedge Dave in between other appointments after she finished with the customer in her chair.

Dave took a seat in the waiting area. Something about Tammy, possibly the nose ring and wild hair color, appealed to him, and he could see that she was keeping an eye on him too as she worked on her customer. Dave knew he would leave the salon with her phone number. But before that happened, the reporter had to see if he could glean some information about Betty Huffmann.

Now Dave could feel the eyes of another woman checking him out carefully. An older woman, pushing seventy-five, Dave guessed, had just come out from under a hair dryer. Her hair was wound tightly around curlers. A vague smell of warm chemicals enveloped her. She looked up at Dave, who sensed that she might be a little uncomfortable with a stranger settling in beside her.

"Don't worry, I don't bite," Dave said, introducing himself. "I can find another chair if you'd like me to."

"My name is Nettie, and I don't bite either," she said, a smile brightening her face. A long blue floral dress peeked out from under her styling bib, paired with nylon stockings rolled down to just below her knee. Floppy slippers, which looked like two hairy puppies, encased her feet.

"You're new in town," Nettie said, resting her *People* magazine in her lap. "Don't believe I've seen you here before."

Dave thought this was a good time to reveal that he worked as a reporter for *The Bay City Blade*. He said he was visiting Pigeon to talk with people in the area about the family tragedy that had occurred on Wild Fowl Bay.

"No kidding, you're a reporter?" Nettie said, her easy, friendly smile returning to her round face. She had a second chin and wrinkles at the corners of her eyes and mouth. "I would never have guessed it. You look more like a pipefitter, complete with the plumber's crack that I noticed while you were at the counter." She tossed the magazine on top of the coffee table in front of them, then reached up with both hands and patted the outside of the curlers to see how warm they were. "You know, my late husband wore a belt, and it's remarkable how efficient it was at holding up his trousers."

Dave laughed loudly enough to draw stares from the other customers in the studio. He liked Nettie already. They chatted freely, and the elderly woman revealed that her husband of forty-seven years had passed on two years before. Her sisters had moved into the farmhouse with her because she could not stand how quiet and lonely the place had become.

A shriek came from the nail corner of the salon. Customers and stylists turned their attention to the source of the whooping cries. "Oh my god, you've got six toes."

"Yeah, well, I hope you're not going to charge me extra for the pedicure," the customer said. "It's just a little bonus pinky toe. They don't charge me extra at the salon in Elkton."

The exchange in the nail corner prompted light laughter, brightening the mood. Dave felt the uplift in spirits opened the door to ask about the Huffmann family, particularly the new widow in the area.

"Nobody knows much about Betty. She was new to these parts when she married Carl," Nettie said. "Not very friendly— secretive."

Dave asked if Betty had become active in her daughter's life at

Laker Schools.

"Minimum involvement—parent-teacher conferences, that's it," she said, scrunching up her face in disapproval. Nettie was a grandparent volunteer at Laker, she said, supervising the lunchroom two days a week and helping in the library when needed. "In fact, rumors have it that Katie's older than she lets on. That girl is too worldly, if you know what I mean, for seventeen years old."

Dave's new friend said Betty had taken an interest in the local book club, which was hosted by the Pigeon District Library the last Tuesday of each month. The club, which consisted of a dozen feisty women and one bored old guy, had welcomed her to their lively discussions.

"My sister and I delivered the book of the month out to her place once," she said. "She invited us in for cookies and coffee in the front parlor. It was the most talkative I'd ever seen her. She mentioned she was planning a trip home to Chicago, which caught me by surprise—I don't know many folks who call the big city home."

Nettie said she'd asked Mrs. Huffmann what living in Chicago was like. It was hard for her to imagine life among so many people—so much noise, so much commotion. The question had prompted Betty to open up, something she did not often do. After a few minutes of small talk about the Windy City, Betty had gone to a bureau drawer in the front room and retrieved a photo album.

"Nice photos. Bright lights. Lots of people," Nettie said. "It was from 1999. I saw a photo of her ex-husband, I guess—it was labeled Charles and Betty Lippman. He looked kind of mousy."

Dave asked if anything else had stood out from the photo album.

Nettie rose from her chair, trying to straighten her back. She needed to stretch but did not want to break her discussion with Dave; she enjoyed sharing what she knew.

"Not one photo of Katie in the whole album," she said. "Edna—that's my little sister—said she noticed the same thing. And all the photos were kind of impersonal, kind of cold. Nobody seemed to be having any fun. Very strange. Betty is an odd one."

"Hey, big guy." Tammy beckoned from her workstation. "You're next. Follow me to the sink. We're going to start by washing that thing on your head."

Dave and Nettie shook hands. "But I can't recall your last name," he said.

"That's because I did not give it to you."

Dave looked surprised.

"I did that on purpose," she said, smiling again. "That way I know I'm not going to see it printed in the paper."

"Well, how will I find you in the future?"

"I'm right here in this chair every Saturday morning," she said. "If you don't see me, then you better check the cemetery."

They laughed, and Dave asked her to wish him well in Tammy's chair.

Chapter 26

Tom Huffmann drove his deceased father's aging farm truck down Crescent Beach Road toward Sand Point. He was hoping to catch Nice Nurse Nora at the Thompson cottage on Sunday afternoon before the family returned to the city and their work lives.

Tom shivered against the cold. The truck's heater did not work well, and temperatures had turned frigid over the weekend. Snow flurries whirled in the wind and made the road surface slippery. The rhythmic pace of the windshield wipers broke the silence in the cab.

Ice had reformed and hardened on the lake. Tom watched ice fishermen wrestling with their gear and venturing out on Wild Fowl Bay. His heart raced. He remembered how cold he had been a week earlier—numb to the bone. He couldn't believe how his life had turned upside down in the course of one week.

The Thompsons were getting ready to break camp when Tom pulled up in their driveway. Gary and the boys were loading the family's two vehicles. Tom noticed the trash was piled in large cans that stood in a wire mesh bin at the edge of the drive for Monday morning pickup.

One object in the bin caught his eye. The cement-filled pipe that Tom had made rested atop old Christmas ornaments that the family had decided to discard. He wondered if the Thompsons had given the pipe a second thought when it was thrown into the junk pile. Tom considered grabbing the pipe and tossing it in the back of the truck, but he was afraid someone in the cottage might see him and ask him about it. He left it alone.

Nora greeted Tom with a big hug. The embrace gave Tom a

feeling of warmth, an ease he had not felt since the last time he'd seen her, when she had visited him in the hospital.

"Tom, what a nice surprise," Nora said. "But we're almost packed up—I don't have even a cup of coffee to offer you."

"No, I'm good." He pulled back from the comfort of Nora's arms. "I was out for a drive, just to do some thinking and kinda sort stuff out. Sand Point is a great place to do that. Figured I'd swing by and see if you were still here."

Gary approached and gave Tom a handshake and pat on the back. He asked how the young man was holding up after the tragedy of the previous week.

"I'm doing okay," Tom said. "Staying with my brother in Bay City right now. We're not sure what's going to happen with the farm. Everything is up in the air." His eyes welled. His stomach churned. For a moment he thought his heart might burst.

The Thompsons watched their young friend struggle with the moment. The neighborhood was quiet; only a woodpecker's rhythmic work off in the distance broke the silence.

After several minutes Tom seemed to regain his composure. "Nora, could I talk with you privately for a few minutes?" he asked. "I know you're getting ready to leave, but there's a couple of things I want you to hear from me."

Nora nodded and led Tom into the cottage, which had already begun to cool with the heat reduced. The living room was dimmed by drawn shades, the furniture covered in sheets.

The two sat down on a covered couch, facing each other. Tom let it fly, bellowing in long sobs. Nora put her hand on his shoulder, hoping to comfort him, but this time her gesture had little effect.

"What is it, Tom?" she kept saying. She handed him a wad of tissue and waited for him to regain control of himself. Tom took a deep breath and mopped at his eyes, now puffy and red.

"I think I may be in some deep trouble," Tom said finally. "Don't know what's going on, but your reporter friend told me the cops have what they think is a weapon that might have been used on my dad out on the ice."

"What? I don't understand," Nora said. She raised her hand to her mouth.

"They found a wrench on the ice—skin and hair on it. Now they're checking DNA to see if it's my dad's." Tom stood up, then sat back down, resting his elbows on his knees. He stared down at the floor.

"I think that deputy is trying to frame me," he said. "I've seen him mooning around Betty. They've been playing around for the last year. They're up to something—I just know it."

"Oh my, my," Nora said, stunned. She did not know how to react or what to say. "I'm shocked."

"I wanted you to hear it from me. Please believe me, I did not kill my dad," Tom said. He faced Nora again, locking in eye contact. "No matter what you hear or read, I did not do it. Lots of stuff might come out, but I am innocent," he said, raising his right hand. "I swear it."

"I believe you," she said, patting his shoulder. But now that he had opened up to her, she wanted more. "What kind of stuff?"

Tom said he had posted a few derogatory comments about his father on Facebook, Twitter, and Snapchat—just a bunch of young guys spouting off. He said he was afraid the deputy might try to use the comments against him.

The two heard the door in the utility room open. Gary came into the cottage but stopped in the kitchen when he received a nod from his wife.

"We're just finishing up, Gary. I'll be with you in a few," Nora said, not taking her eyes off Tom.

She asked Tom if there was anything else he'd like to talk about. He shook his head no, taking a handful of deep breaths. "Thanks for listening," he said. "I had to tell somebody, and I was afraid you'd hear a bunch of crap that's not true."

They walked out toward Gary in the kitchen.

"Everything okay?" Gary asked. "Anything I can do?"

"I'm better now," he replied, then smiled at Nora.

Nora nodded. They hugged again, and Tom left the cottage.

Chapter 27

Amazing how much information, much of it junk, flows through a newsroom every day. Reports, studies, analyses, requests for publicity, unsolicited news releases. Unfortunately a lot of trees have to die to create the mounds of junk.

Nick Steele spent the first two hours of Monday morning sorting through the piles of crap that had been heaped on his desk in the *Blade* newsroom while he was on suspension for a week.

As he pulled up a third large trashcan to the corner of his desk, Greta Norris pushed the play button on her CD player. Country star Toby Keith's "How Do You Like Me Now?!" blared from the loudspeakers. Greta cranked the sound up a few notches.

The double doors leading into the newsroom burst open, and in danced Dave Balz, dressed in his finest blue jean suit, complete with a white shirt and black string tie. The hard heels of his cowboy boots clattered on the tile floor.

But the fancy duds were not the main attraction. The reporter, whom the publisher had nicknamed Harry Balz for his bushy, wild appearance and crude manners, showed off his new hair. As he pranced into the newsroom, Dave used his index fingers, held at chest level, to point to his new look.

Stunned silence and gaping awe might best describe the reactions of Dave's coworkers, including Nick and Greta.

Dave's long, stringy brown-and-gray hair had been replaced with bright-orange curls—a head full of them. The reporter's newfound stylist, the often copied but never duplicated Tamara of Pigeon, had lopped off three inches of hair, thinned it by a quarter, and changed the color to resemble the head mop sported by comedian

Scott "Carrot Top" Thompson.

The new look, totally maintenance-free, pleased Dave. He smiled ear to ear as he danced a country jig right into the middle of the newsroom. Reporters and editors erupted into applause at the bulky reporter's new look and locks.

The festive mood, however, came to a sudden halt when the C-Man clapped his large paws together, snatching the attention of all who had focused on the grand entrance.

"What the hell is going on here?" the editor said. "Balz, what are you doing? Is the circus in town, or what? Have you lost your mind? My god, you look hideous."

The smile fell from Dave's face. Someone shut off the music, and the reporter stopped dancing in the aisles of the newsroom. He knew the bright-orange hair might have been a tad over the top, but he liked what Tammy had done for him. He figured the brightness would come down a notch or two over time.

Just then Diane Givens, the publisher who was also known as the Castrator for her abrupt manner when it came to discipline, walked into the newsroom. She sauntered up to Dave, who stood alone now, and looked him up and down.

"I like it—a vast improvement," she pronounced. "But then again, you were so rock-bottom low that the only place you could go was up."

"Diane, please," the C-Man said. "You're not helping matters."

The publisher shrugged and headed for the door leading to the advertising department. Most of the reporters and editors returned to their work, but a few rushed to Dave's side to get a close-up of the new look.

The C-Man called for Nick to meet with him in his office. He said he wanted an update on the ice-fishing story. "And make sure you bring Bozo with you," he said.

"You know, I take exception to that comment," Dave said, closing Clapper's door as they entered his office. "Bozo's hair was bright red. My color is called Auburn Sunset."

"Yeah, right. Okay, you two tell me what I need to know about that ice-fishing death out in the Thumb. Sounds pretty open and shut to me. Patricide. Happens far more often than most people think—especially when big money's involved."

Dave nodded and pushed a pile of old newspapers off a chair so he could have a seat. Dust fluttered in the air, and the reporter ducked to the side so it would not land on his new 'do.

Nick pushed back against his boss. "Hold on, hold on. There's a lot going on here," he said, sitting down in the only open chair in the office. "All the fingers are pointing at Tom Huffmann, but I'm not convinced yet."

Nick gave his boss a quick review of what he'd learned that had not been reported, particularly the wrench found near the scene. "If it turns out to have Carl's tissue, then the whole story changes dramatically," he said. He explained that he'd already talked with Tom and Richard Huffmann about the wrench and tissue, but that Tom had flatly denied having anything to do with his father's death.

"And here's what doesn't make sense to me." Nick stood up to emphasize his point to the boss. "If Tom made a weapon and carried it out on the ice with him to kill his dad, then why would he use a big-ass crescent wrench instead? I found the cement-filled pipe in his wet ice-fishing gear, so it's pretty clear he had it on him the whole time. Just doesn't add up for me."

Another interesting bit of information, Nick said, was that Carl had met Betty at a Midwest seed corn conference.

"Hey, I understand love at first sight and all that stuff, but why would a big-city woman go to a farmers' convention in Des Moines unless her intention was to do some gold-digging?"

The managing editor nodded, then looked at Dave, studying the top of his head from close range. "What have you got—besides issues with how you look? Is that a burn mark on your scalp?"

"Ah, kinda. The curlers stayed in too long, and Tammy might have used more chemicals than she needed to," Dave said. "But it looks much better today than it did Saturday afternoon."

Clapper shook his head. "Did you get anything worthwhile on Saturday?"

Dave revealed what he'd learned from Nettie, which piqued the C-Man's interest. Dave was so encouraged by the editor's reaction that he decided to dive in and suggest a trip to Chicago to track down more on the backgrounds of Betty and Katie, whom they knew very little about.

"No, nobody is going to Chicago just yet," Clapper said, shaking his head. "I still think it's a case of patricide. And I think you people are spending way too much time on this story. Let's see what the justice system has to say about it. I figure a jury out in the Thumb will have no trouble finding the wayward Huffmann son guilty."

Nick pleaded his case to the managing editor. "Give us some more time. We're digging hard, and we've got to look behind some more closed doors." The reporter could see by the expression on Clapper's face that he and Dave were winning the argument. He went in for the kill, telling the editor exactly what Nick knew he wanted to hear. "Even if I'm wrong about Tom Huffmann, it will be great reading. Look what happened to this all-American family."

Clapper finally relented. "Okay, go ahead and work it some more, but you better come up with some great stuff. This newspaper does not publish itself every day," he said. "I need some good copy, so go get the story."

The C-Man did not rule out a trip to the Windy City, but he wanted Dave to continue checking on the two women long-distance for now. "Have Greta give you a hand," he told him. "Let's see what we can dig out on them in the next few days. Nick, you're running hot on Tom Huffmann. Stick with him. Is the prosecutor going to issue charges?"

"Hard to say. Billington is a nervous Nellie," Nick said. "I think it all hangs on the DNA tests. We should know anytime."

Clapper told both men to keep him updated on developments, and he suggested Dave stay out of beauty salons in the future.

Laughing, Nick returned to his desk, where he found a note from Greta. She was on her way to Bad Axe because she had received word that Tom Huffmann had been arrested, with arraignment scheduled for that afternoon.

The speed at which the arrest had come surprised Nick. But with formal charges in the works, he could put together his story for Tuesday's paper. It would include Tom Huffmann's denial that he had anything to do with his dad's death. Greta would add the formalities and—hopefully—quotes from the prosecutor and sheriff's department.

Nick tried calling the Huffmann brothers. No response from Tom, of course, but Richard answered. He said Tom was being held in the Huron County Jail facing first-degree, or premeditated, murder charges. His older brother said jail guards had Tom on suicide watch because he was so distraught.

"Looks like he will be in there for a while too," Richard said. "Bail is set at $100,000, but it might as well be a million bucks. We don't have much dough, and we can't borrow against the farm because Betty has got it all locked up."

Nick detected defeat in Richard's voice, like he believed Tom was up against insurmountable odds. The reporter asked if he had any positive developments to report.

Richard said Bob Skinner had been appointed by the district

judge at arraignment to represent Tom. Skinner had told the brothers that he hoped to get the case tossed out during the evidentiary hearing later that week.

"Skinner thinks the prosecution's case is flimsy," he said. "No direct evidence. No witnesses and nothing to tie Tom to that wrench. It's a Sears Craftsman, which means it could have come out of any one of a thousand toolboxes in the Thumb."

Nick jotted notes. He told Richard he thought the origin of the wrench was a very good point for Skinner to pursue.

"Tom says he didn't do it, and I believe him," Richard said, taking a positive and more aggressive tone. "He thinks Betty and that sheriff's deputy, the one they call Booger, are trying to frame him."

Nick asked Richard to stay in touch. He said that he was doing his best to find out more on the origins of Betty and Katie.

As he clicked off his cell, Nick motioned for Dave, who was on the phone with Greta, to come over to his desk. He needed his sounding board again.

"Just talked with Richard," Nick said, then summarized what he'd heard. "The brothers are saying this is all a setup by the stepmom and Deputy Ratchett, that Tom is innocent. The C-Man seems fairly convinced it's a case of patricide. What's your take? What's your gut say?"

"My gut says it's lunchtime," Dave said, trying to look as serious as he could.

"Come on, Dave, get real, will ya?" Nick said, rolling his eyes. "How does this strike you?"

The reporter grimaced. He had two immediate reactions, he said. First, he was suspicious of Betty and her motives; the way she'd handled herself at the funeral, Dave thought, indicated she had done a lot of planning and scheming. The revocation of the prenup and the way she'd sprung it on the brothers so that it would be captured on camera gave him the creeps because it had happened as though it had been choreographed. When he finished tracking down her history in Chicago, Dave hoped to have a better idea of how she and her daughter fit into the story.

Secondly, Dave said, he was struggling to accept the whole concept of patricide himself. As Clapper had noted, there were plenty of examples of children plotting to murder their parents. But it was totally foreign to Dave, whose dad had been killed in Vietnam before it even was a war. The reporter sat on a corner of Nick's desk and sighed. "1959," he said. "I never knew my dad—you know that. Do you have any idea what I would have done to have had a father, even a lousy one? My mom brought home 'uncles of the month.' So when I heard those guys at O'Hare's the other day congratulating Tom for dancing on his dad's casket, it really hit me. Didn't sleep much that night thinking about it."

Dave was getting emotional, which did not happen very often. Nick patted him on the shoulder and said he'd had the same feelings at O'Hare's but had not brought it up at the time.

"Didn't seem appropriate then, but the conversation made me nauseous," he said. Dave listened with his head down. "I loved my dad," Nick said. "Miss him every day, so I don't get it either. I'm with you."

The two reporters sat on the desk side by side. Neither said a word. They didn't have to.

After a few minutes Nick spoke first. "Sometimes this job forces you to go to places you don't want to visit," he said. "That's just one of the reasons I love it so."

Chapter 28

Corn was king in Des Moines, Iowa, but so was just about every other aspect of American farming. Carl Huffmann had loved the great Midwest city and its culture. He visited Des Moines at least once every year.

The farmer had never missed a chance to learn more about his family's profession. And he'd enjoyed rubbing elbows with other farmers—especially when they flocked to Des Moines from all over the world for one of the dozens of conferences and exhibits produced in the city each year.

Figuring out which conferences Carl had attended in Des Moines seemed daunting to Dave, who spent all of Tuesday morning calling corn growing organizations and companies. His reporting buddy, Nick, did the same thing on the other side of the newsroom.

They hoped to pick up a lead on how and when Carl met Betty, but they were getting nowhere. Dave also tried verifying the information he'd picked up at the Shear Crazy Salon. But most leads on Charles and Betty Lippman in Chicago had dried up.

Finally he found an obituary in the *Chicago Tribune* for Charles in 2001. The obit said the Chicago native—a department store manager—had died while making electrical repairs to his home in Orland Park, located southwest of the city. The death notice also said Betty, his wife of six years, was his only survivor. No mention in the obit of a child or stepchild, which Dave found interesting. Why wouldn't Katie be mentioned, he wondered, in an obituary?

Dave's cell phone rang. It was Tamara of Pigeon. As predicted, Dave the Ladykiller Balz, had indeed walked away from Shear Crazy with Tammy's number. He smiled at the sight of it, clicking the call on.

"So what do your friends think?" Tammy said before Dave could extend a greeting. "Tell me the truth."

"Doesn't matter what they think," Dave said. "Only matters what I think, and I love it. Several have commented that getting rid of the gray makes me look younger, which I hadn't really thought much about."

"Glad to hear it," she said. "Just thought I'd check up on you."

Dave decided to ask Tammy who in the Pigeon area might know which seed corn conference Carl Huffmann had attended.

"Ain't no secrets in a small town," she said. "I got a friend who works in the office over at the co-op. They know everything about everybody. If I get anything, I'll shoot you a text."

Within fifteen minutes, Dave's cell dinged with an incoming text: "Association of American Corn Growers meeting every February. Carl a regular."

Dave thanked Tammy and texted her back that he owed her dinner.

"All right!" she responded. "Gonna hold you to it."

On the AACG website, Dave and Nick found a board of directors, officers, and public relations specialists, as well as tons of information about corn and farming. The association's committee assignments revealed that Carl was a regular volunteer, holding key positions in research and development and in membership training. Carl would be well-known among members—which made the reporters ecstatic. They divided up the names and started calling.

Nick and Dave worked all afternoon, connecting with one board member or officer after another. Many had heard of Carl because he was such an active participant in the association, but no one knew much about him personally.

Finally Nick connected with Woodrow Tipton, a recording

secretary for the organization who also served as registrar of the conference.

"Well, hell yes, I know Carl," he said. "See him here every year. Great guy. We usually have breakfast together at least two or three times during the weeklong conference."

Nick informed Woodrow that Carl had passed away while out ice fishing with his son. He did not add any other details.

"Oh, damn. I'm really sorry to hear that. Damn!" the man said. Nick could hear genuine surprise and disappointment in his voice. "Great guy. Lots of terrific stories, and one hell of a good farmer too. Took a lot of pride in that."

Nick shared the positive aspects of Carl's funeral, omitting the wild drama that had made the deceased's farewell the talk of the Thumb. "Had a real nice turnout," he said. "All the local farmers and town dignitaries attended the services. It was quite a sight to see."

Then Woodrow asked a question that made Nick's day. "How's Betty taking it? She okay?"

Nick tried to contain his glee. He threw a pencil at Dave, who was working the phones at another desk. When his buddy looked up after taking the projectile in the arm, Nick gave him a big smile and a thumbs-up.

"Ah, Betty is doing as well as could be expected," Nick said. "Did you know Betty very well, Woodrow?"

"Call me Woody—everybody does," he said. Nick listened closely to Woody's slow Southern drawl, which made him think of Tennessee. "I was with Carl when he met Betty, you know. She was at the conference with some girlfriends, some good-lookin' gals, real head-turners, if I recall correctly."

"Betty was with friends at the conference?" Nick asked. He thought that was interesting—and wanted details. "How did they actually meet, Woody?"

"Kinda funny how they stumbled into one another," he said. "Accidental, really. We were having dinner in the conference ballroom. Betty—Betty Tate, she was then—and her friends were going to sit at a table nearby, but they were short one chair. Betty came up and explained their dilemma and asked if the girls could use the extra seat at our table.

"I told her they were welcome to take the chair," Woody said, describing the meeting and exchange. "But Carl jumped up and carried the chair over to their table himself. They talked for a spell, and then Carl came back, grinnin' like he just got done lickin' pudding off a spoon."

"The what?"

"Ah, nothing. Just an expression for a moment of joy."

"I take it that was the beginning of their romance."

"Pretty much. Saw them together every day after that. Then the next year Carl told me that Betty had visited him at his place in Michigan. Next thing I knew, they were hitched."

Nick asked if Woody had met Betty's daughter, Katie. The registrar said he did not know Betty had a daughter—she had only mentioned her friends. Woody said Betty's girlfriends had found fellas by the end of the conference too. "Real nice guys," the man said. "One farmed in Wisconsin, and the other was from Ohio. Walter Dupinski of Prairie Farm and Edgar Truscott of Amanda. Haven't seen 'em since."

Chapter 29

Nice Nurse Nora called Nick early Wednesday morning. The reporter had just gotten off the phone with Richard Huffmann, who had told Nick his brother wanted to speak with him in person as soon as possible. That request had caught Nick off guard; at this stage in the legal process, he'd pretty much given up on getting a full interview with Tom.

Nora was delighted to hear the news. "We've talked several times on the phone since his arrest," she said. "He and Richard believe Tom is being railroaded by the deputy. Tom wants his story to get out before he ends up in court. I encouraged him to contact you—to tell the full story."

Nick was a bit surprised at Nora's ringing endorsement. He wanted an interview with Tom, but he also wanted the young man to come clean. The reporter was a little concerned that Nora was being overly trusting and that Tom had hoodwinked her. He asked the nurse why she believed him.

"Call it intuition if you want," she said. "I can see the truth in his eyes."

Nick had trouble swallowing that notion. Over the years he'd looked into the eyes of stone-cold killers who'd denied their guilt and showed no trace of it even through the portals to their souls.

"What do you think, Nick?" Nora said. "I believe Tom's being sincere, but I also know charges would not have been filed if they didn't have some evidence against him."

"Not sure what to think. I'm trying my best not to form an opinion—going to see him at the jail this afternoon," Nick said. "Either way, I don't think he's telling us the full story. I'm hoping he opens up when I sit down with him."

"Me too, Nick. Hope it all works out for him. Good luck with your interview."

Nora was about to click off the phone when Nick remembered his lost gloves.

Nora said her sons had found the gloves and some other personal items after the rescuers had left the property. She said she'd put everything on a table on the back porch, figuring those who'd lost things would come looking for their stuff.

Nick said he would take a look when he was in the Thumb later that day. It also meant he now had a legitimate reason to go back to her place and poke around for the cement-filled pipe. He thanked her for calling and said he would be back in touch.

As the reporter packed up for his trip to the Thumb, Greta stopped by his desk, offering to help in any way she could—even if it meant working after hours on her own time.

Nick thanked her for being such a good team player on a difficult story. He updated Greta with the new information they had gathered on Betty Huffmann and advised her to check in with Dave, who was working the phones. If he didn't need help, then Nick had a couple of ideas for her to chase.

Next the C-Man motioned for Nick to stop in his office. The editor wanted a quick update before the reporter disappeared again. "Nick, what's going to come up at that evidentiary hearing?" he asked. "Has the prosecutor got some surprises up his sleeve?"

"Not sure. We've heard he may have some social media posts," Nick said, sitting down in Clapper's office to explain. "Could also have some witnesses from among Tom's friends. But I got a call that Tom wants to talk with me at the jail, so I'm heading to Bad Axe now," he said. "Dave and Greta are working the phones from here. Will let you know if I get some kind of amazing revelation."

Nick left the newsroom before he could be delayed again.

Once outside the city, he relaxed. The wide-open spaces and flat farm fields of the Thumb gave Nick the chance to think without the distractions of the newsroom. He was glad Nora had mentioned that Tom thought he was being set up to take the fall in his father's death, a theory Richard had already brought up. He was sure they would talk about that when Nick arrived at the jail for the interview.

Nick hoped his conversation with the youngest Huffmann son would be productive. The reporter needed answers, and he hadn't had much luck on Betty Huffmann and her daughter. Dave was still on it, but Nick had a feeling they were missing something—that they weren't looking in the right places.

To Nick, the initial meeting between Betty and Carl in Des Moines was too convenient to be purely coincidental. He also wondered why she had used the name Betty Tate if she was previously a Lippman. And what about MacDonald—who he presumed was Katie's dad? He wasn't sure how these men fit into the picture. It was also possible, he thought, that Katie was not Betty's daughter at all, but he did not know how they might be connected instead.

That reminded Nick of Carl's secret life and his real daughters in Caro. He needed to find out when Betty had learned of the scandal and what the fallout was. Nick wondered if that might have been the leverage Betty used to get Carl to revoke the prenup. The Huffmann household, he was discovering, was full of secrets and shady backgrounds.

Nick pulled off to the side of the road to make a note to follow up with the three sisters out at the German restaurant. He thought they might have done some of their own investigating into the backgrounds of the two new women who'd ended up in Carl's homestead farmhouse. From what Nick had seen, Carlina was a bulldog, and he was willing to bet she would have plenty of dirt on Betty.

Nick checked his watch and decided he had enough time to stop at the cottage on Sand Point before making his scheduled interview at the jail in Bad Axe. He turned onto Crescent Beach Road and whizzed by the mostly darkened lakefront homes, vacated—for now—by snowbirds.

When Nick pulled into the Thompsons' driveway, he spotted the items Nora had piled on the table on the back porch—his gloves among them.

He was also delighted to see that the trash collection had not taken place on the secluded street, which was not unusual during off-season winter months. As he backed out of the driveway, Nick took care not to run into the mound of junk piled around the trash bin. Immediately he noticed the chunk of cement-filled pipe he'd found among Tom's wet outerwear on the night of the drowning. He stopped the Firebird and pulled the pipe out of the bin. It was as heavy as he recalled, and capped at one end. He pulled out his cell phone and took a photo of the pipe. Then he tossed the pipe on the floor in front of the passenger's seat and made for the jail.

Chapter 30

On Wednesday afternoon Deputy Ratchett knocked on the side door of the Huffmann homestead, hoping that Betty would be home and give him entry.

"Sweet Cheeks, please, you gotta let me in," Jay-Bob said, stomping the snow off his boots. He could see his breath in the cold air as he spoke. "I really need to talk to you. Pretty please!"

The deputy could hear movement in the kitchen, and he stepped forward, excited at the idea of talking to Betty again. They had only seen each other briefly since Carl's funeral. But his glee changed to disdain when the door popped open and Katie stood glaring at him.

"I ain't your Sweet Cheeks," Katie said. "What the hell do you want?"

"Need to talk with Betty right away," the deputy said, peering into the kitchen behind Katie. He thought he could see the shadow of someone else in the room with her. "Is that her?"

Jay-Bob pushed the door open. It was not Betty but a young man in the kitchen, leaning against the sink. His facial features were dimmed by the backlight coming from the window behind him.

"Betty ain't here, and you're not welcome," Katie said. "You got no right to force your way into the house."

Jay-Bob ignored her and the rude reception. He had never liked Katie much, and even less so now. He focused his attention on the stranger, asking the man to identify himself.

"Probably better for you not to know my name," the guy said. "But it's safe to say that I ain't your Sweet Cheeks either. I've seen Betty many times—never thought her face was all that pretty."

"Don't think he's talking about the cheeks on Betty's face," Katie said. She and the stranger laughed. Jay-Bob did not.

The sound of a vehicle coming up the driveway prompted all three to look out the window. It was the new Lincoln Navigator. Relieved, the deputy left the young people inside and went out to the driveway to greet Betty.

The widow wasted no time letting Jay-Bob know she was not pleased to see him. She started giving him hell before the Lincoln's driver's side door slammed shut.

"You know you're not supposed to come out here anymore," she said. "Too dangerous. I told you to contact me on the secure cell only in emergencies. This better be one hell of an emergency."

The deputy explained that Prosecutor Billington was getting nervous about the evidentiary hearing coming up.

"Now that the charges have been filed, he's going to have to tip his hand and show the best evidence he's got to the judge," Jay-Bob said. "He asked me to nose around and see if I could come up with more info or witnesses to testify."

"I gave you everything I had—all his writings," she said. "And you got a look at his room. What else do you want?"

Jay-Bob urged her to scour the house again. He said he also wanted to look around the garage and toolsheds to see if he could find anything of Tom's that might look like he was making some kind of weapon.

Plus, the deputy said, he just plain missed seeing Betty.

"Now, don't go acting like some lovesick puppy," she said, moving closer to Jay-Bob. She poked him in the chest with her index finger. "Go ahead and look around if you want. That's reason enough for you to be out here. But when you leave do not, I repeat, DO NOT come back. Once again, I will let you know when I think it's okay for us to be together."

"Aw, Sweet Cheeks, you're torturing me!" His voice was child-like—almost whining.

"Cut that shit out," Betty said. "Suck it up. Stop calling me that and start acting like a man. We've got a long way to go before we're clear. I am not going to allow you to screw this up."

The deputy told Betty that her words had cut him to the core. He said he would check the outbuildings and be on his way, but he asked her to look one more time for diaries or journals. Jay-Bob couldn't resist asking about the stranger inside the farmhouse too—the sight of him had made the deputy jealous and a little suspicious of what was going on out here at the farm.

"Just a friend of Katie's. Forget you saw him." She stomped back into the house.

The garage was dark, and the deputy fumbled along the wall until he found a light switch. The place was loaded with tools and equipment—no surprise for any farm garage in the area. But he also noticed a large commercial wood chipper sitting in a corner. It didn't look like it had been used in a while. Off to the side, in front of the entry door, the deputy spotted what he was really interested in knowing more about: a red four-wheel drive Chevy pickup, covered in enough mud to hide most of its bright color.

The deputy walked around the vehicle. He did not recognize it as one of the many pickups in the area, and it was too fancy for a farm truck. Jay-Bob looked in the cab. A shotgun and a half-dozen shells lay on the floor across the driver's and passenger's sides within easy reach of the driver. He wondered if it was loaded. Lots of farmers carried shotguns in their trucks, but it was against the law to drive around with a loaded weapon. He reached in through an open window and opened the center console. Drugs—pills in an unmarked bottle—and an Altoids tin containing white powder. He could smell the remains of burned pot. An empty vodka bottle lay on the floor of the rear cab.

"Not good," Jay-Bob said out loud. The deputy pulled out his cell phone and snapped a photograph of the VIN through the front windshield. He also went to the back of the truck for a photo of the license plate.

The bed of the truck, he noticed, was loaded with fishing gear. The deputy was just about to look under the tarp in the back when the garage door opened. It was Betty.

"You won't find any of Tom's stuff in that truck," she said, holding up a notebook, which she said she'd discovered between her stepson's mattress and box spring. "Please look for what you came after, then leave."

Jay-Bob gave the notebook a quick scan, then tucked it under his arm. He thanked her and said he was heading back to Bad Axe. He leaned toward Betty and puckered his lips to give her a smooch good-bye, but she pushed him away and walked back into the farm-house.

That angered the deputy. He got in his cruiser, but at the end of the driveway he stopped to check the images on his cell phone. He emailed pictures of the VIN and the license plate number to the desk deputy on duty, asking for a check on ownership—and he requested a rush.

"He's not going to be a stranger for long," Jay-Bob said to him-self as he pulled out on the highway toward Bad Axe.

Chapter 31

Attorney Bob Skinner met Nick at the visitor's entrance to the Huron County Jail. Normally visitors spoke with inmates through a vented plexiglass window, but Tom's attorney had arranged for the two to meet in an interview room instead. Nick would be searched before speaking with Tom, but they would be able to talk openly.

"Now, I want you to know up front that I have advised Tom—in writing, and I had him sign it—that he should not speak with you before trial," Skinner said. "Told him there is nothing to be gained from talking to you from a legal standpoint, and a whole lot to lose."

"I'm surprised that he contacted me." Nick pulled out the voice recorder he planned to use during the interview and checked the breast pocket of his jacket to make sure the printed photo of the cement-filled pipe he'd taken with his cell was where it was supposed to be. "But I'm glad he did. I think there's much more to this story than we know."

The reporter followed the attorney into a long beige hallway, where a deputy greeted them outside the first doorway. Though he'd already been searched once, Nick set his laptop and recorder on the floor and held his hands outstretched at shoulder height. The deputy checked him and his gear out.

Tom was sitting at a table inside the small cubicle. His hands were cuffed and manacled to his waist. Chains attached to his feet ran to the belt around his waist. The inmate wore orange coveralls and a white T-shirt. He did not rise to greet Nick, but the reporter stuck out his hand. They shook, making Tom's shackles rattle.

Nick thanked Tom for contacting him and agreeing to the interview. The inmate said he wanted to clear the air.

"I'm going to tell you everything," he said, settling back into his chair—steel, with a foam seat. The matching gray steel table was just big enough for Nick to set up his laptop, recorder, and notebook. "I want my side of the story out there for all to read," Tom said. "If the court and a jury decide to send me to prison, possibly for life, then so be it."

"Hold on, hold on," Nick said, flicking on the recorder and opening his laptop. He pulled out a pen and set up his notebook. "You're off and running already, and I haven't got everything turned on yet. Let's go over the ground rules first."

"Okay, shoot," Tom said, laughing out loud. "Oops, poor choice of words, since I'm in here for murder."

Nick did not respond. Instead he spoke directly to the recorder, giving the time and date and noting that this was the beginning of an interview with Thomas Huffmann inside the Huron County Jail. He clarified that all questions and answers would be on the record and that none would be omitted.

The reporter decided to start the interview with a question that he had asked Tom previously. He wondered if Tom would answer in the same way as before. "Did you kill your father?"

"No, I did not, but I am probably responsible for his death."

That response surprised Nick, but he tried not to show it. "Please continue."

Tom led off by going back to the beginning. He recounted a childhood that was largely unhappy but that had become absolutely unbearable after his mother passed away. His father, he said, had turned into an angry, ranting bully, driving away his older brothers and making his life a nightmare.

"I would lie in bed at night thinking of how I might kill him," he said. "I checked books on poisons out of the library. I made notes from every crime TV show—*Law and Order* was my favorite. Learned a lot of good ways for people to die."

Tom said he'd written about the subject in his daily diary and later had filled several journals with his feelings. He'd used social media too, he said, though his posts there were mostly impulsive rages.

"But saying is one thing, and actually doing is another," he said. "So yeah, I talked about it a lot. And I'll bet the prosecutor has got some of my old friends lined up to testify against me. But that's okay. I knew what I was doing."

Tom said he'd stayed on the farm, trying to hold on until his dad retired, but his old man had simply become meaner as the years passed. The last straw for Tom was the wind turbines. The two had fought constantly over the giant windmills and their role in the community, as well as other matters important to the continued success and future of the Huffmann farm.

When Carl would not yield, Tom said, he had decided to take the old guy out. Tom had begun actively planning it as early as last fall. His idea was to wait until the lake froze over, take his dad out ice fishing, and then do him in while no one was around. Everyone would think it was a horrible accident, and Tom could get on with his life.

"I even made a club to pop him with," Tom said, almost bragging that his plot was so thoroughly thought out.

"Is this it?" Nick drew out the photo of the cement-filled pipe. "When I first saw it, the pipe was tangled in your wet fishing gear at the Thompsons' place."

Tom seemed surprised. "Yup, that looks like it, but I saw it in the trash on Sunday. How'd you get a photo of it?"

"Stopped there today to pick up my lost gloves and spotted it in the trash when I was pulling out of the driveway," Nick said. He asked Tom if he'd struck his dad with the pipe.

"No," Tom said. "I had the hole in the ice cut extra big so the SOB would fit through it, but I just couldn't bring myself to do it. The old man started talking about Mom—my real mom, not that nasty bitch Betty. Old times, when me and my brothers were little. Then he brought up all the old Christmas celebrations we had. That's when I saw the Christmas tree lights flicker on and off at the Sand Point cottage. Just couldn't finish the job."

Tom said he'd put the chunk of pipe back in his belt, and they'd picked up their fishing gear and decided to go ashore before it became too dark. That's when they had broken through the ice.

"Yup, the ice made some real loud pops, then started giving way right under us," Tom said. "The water was over our heads." Tom described how they had helped each other out of the water and how his dad had broken through the ice again. "He encouraged me to keep going toward the Christmas tree lights on Sand Point—said he was going to swim back to the sandbar where we had gotten out before," Tom said. He fidgeted in his seat, and Nick thought he looked uncomfortable talking about the final time he'd seen his dad alive.

"That was the last I saw of him," Tom said, crossing his arms, which made his chains rattle again. "At the time, I figured he would be okay, and I was going to get help. In my mind he was simply too tough and mean to die. I kept wandering around on the ice, frozen and dazed, until I finally made it to the cottage by following the lights."

Tom said he'd seen no one else out on the ice. "It was all about surviving at that point," he said.

The reporter asked the inmate about the cut on Carl's head. He wanted to know if Tom had in any way caused his dad to hit his head on the 4-wheelers while they flopped in the water.

Tom shook his head. "No. I did not see any kind of cut on my dad, or any blood," he said. "You saw my wet coveralls at the cottage.

No blood on anything."

Nick paused and checked his recorder. He asked Tom about the crescent wrench. "Rescuers found a wrench out on the ice near where you and your dad went into the water. It had human tissue on it that the state police crime lab determined belonged to your dad. Do you know anything about that wrench or how it got your dad's tissue on it?"

"No, that's all news to me," Tom said. Nick thought he sounded defiant. "Not aware of any of that."

Nick nodded but was curious whether Tom thought differently about what had happened, now that he'd had time to reflect. "Are you sorry your dad is gone? Do you wish it had turned out differently?"

"No, I'm not sorry he's dead, but it was wrong for me to plot against him," Tom said. "I was stupid and foolish and selfish. That's why I'm taking full responsibility for what happened. I had my dad out there. I put him in that situation and he died. It's on me, and I am willing to accept the punishment I am given," he said, the chains clinking as he raised his hands and spread them flat on the table. "No appeals after trial. If a jury of my peers sends me to prison, then that's the bed I made, and I will sleep in it."

"Even if you get life?"

"Even if I get life."

Nick thanked Tom for the interview, explaining that he would be covering the trial for *The Blade*. He asked Tom to contact him through Richard if he wanted to talk again. The inmate raised his cuffed hands. They shook, and Nick left the room.

Nick had mixed feelings as he left the county jail. It was a great interview, he thought, but it amounted to a public confession—taped and on the record. He wondered if Tom would regret his statements. Certainly they would not be admissible in court, but Tom's original intentions and plans to kill his father would weigh heavily in the court of public opinion.

As soon as Nick was back inside the Firebird, he rang Dave. "Well," he said, "that crazy bastard just pretty much sent himself to prison."

Chapter 32

When Nick arrived back in the *Blade* newsroom on Thursday morning, Dave was waiting for him. They had big news to share.

Nick put his laptop bag on top of his desk, but Dave would not let him unpack. The older reporter grabbed Nick by the arm.

"You are not going to believe this," Dave said, leading Nick to an area where they would not be heard or interrupted. Once they were in the hallway by the men's room, he looked both ways before continuing, trying hard to contain his excitement. "The names of the farmers you had me check out—well, they're dead."

"What?"

"You heard me. They're dead. Fatal farm accidents about a year apart," Dave said. "Talked to funeral home directors in both towns. The accidents are similar in nature—one got fried and one torn apart, but both were killed while working on farm machinery."

"No shit," Nick said. "Both of them?"

"Yup, but that's not all," Dave said, his voice harried and halting. "Get this. Since they died, their wives sold off all their land and equipment and took off."

"What do you mean, they took off?"

"From what the funeral home directors told me—independent of one another—the same thing happened in both cases. The husbands died, and the wives cleaned up, then disappeared. Nobody has seen or heard from them since they left town."

"Great stuff, Dave. Keep digging," Nick said, encouraging Dave to go all out. They agreed that if they could find those women and see what had become of them, they might be on to something big.

When Nick returned to his desk, he spotted Gordon hovering in his area of the newsroom, reading the personnel crap posted on a bulletin board. The two had not talked since Nick returned to the office from suspension.

Following the managing editor's advice, Nick had steered clear of the intern; he had no intention of giving Morton Reynolds a reason to whack him again. He also did not want the kid going back to his daddy to complain about Nick being mean to him in the newsroom. Sure, they'd bumped into each other in the *Blade* building, but their conversations had not extended beyond simple greetings.

Today, however, it seemed like the intern had other ideas.

"Hey, Nick, wondered if I could talk to you for a couple minutes," Gordon said, his voice just above a whisper. He had not looked Nick in the eye since he'd hurled in the reporter's beloved Firebird. "I've been meaning to apologize, but I didn't know quite how to do it."

"No need to, Gordon," Nick said. "It's probably best to forget about the whole thing. Sometimes things get a bit out of hand."

"Bullshit, Nick. I'm sorry for screwing up out there and getting you in hot water," he said, moving closer to Nick's desk. "And on top of everything else, I blew the assignment. You tried to help me, and I failed you and the paper."

Nick was impressed. Without prompting the kid had 'fessed up and admitted he was wrong, something that Nick didn't think he was mature enough to do. Maybe there was hope for him, the reporter thought.

Gordon also apologized for his dad. He said he knew his father sometimes overreached when it came to anything involving his only son. That's the way it had been his whole life, the intern said.

"I was never going to be able to live up to what he expected from me. I was never going to be Mr. Wing Tips Button-Down-Collar Banker," he said, shaking his head. "That's just not me. So I became the screw-up, goof-off son. Always in trouble all the way through high school and college. Always a disappointment."

Nick nodded, trying to stay neutral, stay positive. He did not know how to respond to Gordon's openness. "Hey, lots of different kinds of father and son relationships out there," he said. "Sounds like yours is still evolving."

"Well, I had to get away from him and out from under him," he said. "That's why I went in a totally different direction with journalism. Now I've got to get serious about it before I screw this totally up."

Nick wanted to encourage the young guy. He asked him what had happened to him during his assignment on Wild Fowl Bay. "What threw you off track? How did you get so messed up so fast?" he asked, settling back into his chair. "You were totally wrecked when I found you at the Bluewater Inn."

"I met this really cool guy named Trevor," the intern said. "We started out talking about ice fishing, but he didn't really know too much about it. Said he was from the city and was still learning about country life."

"Who had the drugs?" Nick asked.

"We both did," Gordon said. "I had a little coke and he had some too, but he also had pills. We did a little, shot the breeze. He said he was a gun and knife collector, and started bragging about it when he found out I was a reporter. Then we smoked a little, drank a little, and the next thing you know, I'm in Caseville at the bar."

"Hey, well, live and learn," Nick said. "We all make mistakes. Hell, I've sure made my share. But I would caution against using drugs. I've never seen anything good come from drug use—casual or otherwise"

He asked if Gordon had heard from Trevor since the day they'd met at Mud Creek. The intern said he had been invited to visit the guy at the farm where he worked but had decided to hold off on the idea.

"Who knows, that might have turned out to be a good story too," Nick said, trying to make the best of an awkward situation. On the other hand, he did not want the kid to wander back into his story. He encouraged him to keep looking for an angle that would help him learn the trade. "Collecting is big-time these days. Lots of folks interested in guns and knives too," he said.

Gordon smiled and stuck out his hand, and Nick shook it. The look on the kid's face said that he was glad he'd talked with the older reporter.

Chapter 33

Katie helped her friend hook the wood chipper up to the back of his Chevy pickup. They were moving it from the garage to the other side of the Huffmann homestead's huge barn. There they would test run the machine and place a manure spreader under its exit chute to catch the chopped-up chips.

While they worked outside, Betty cleaned up the kitchen. She planned to cook Jay-Bob's favorite meal: fried fresh catfish, hash brown potatoes with minced onion, German coleslaw, homemade bread, johnnycake, and chocolate pudding. It would be a dinner that the deputy would always remember. It would also be his last.

Once the food was started, she picked up the secure cell phone the two had agreed to use only in emergencies. Then she punched in the numbers and waited for Jay-Bob to answer. He didn't.

"Aw shit!" she said aloud. "Where the hell is he? He's always hanging around when I don't want him, and then when I do need him he doesn't pick up."

Betty returned to the stove and the food that was slowly simmering to a delicious summation. The deputy had served his purpose, but now he was making her nervous. She was afraid he would blow the whole deal.

After several minutes the secure cell rang. Betty was so relieved that the headache crawling up the back of her skull suddenly disappeared. She took a deep breath and answered. "Hi Ace, glad you called me back."

"What's up?" he said, his voice edgy and cautious and perhaps a little hurt. " You were pretty nasty to me when I saw you at the farm the other day."

"You're right. It's the stress," she said, doing her best to sound contrite, though that was not her nature in the least. "Carl's funeral, the mess with Tom and his brothers, all the things we're trying to do to get the farm in shape. Overwhelming, really. Sorry I took it out on you."

"Are you really?"

"Yes, Ace, and to make it up to you I'm cooking up your favorite dinner right now. Should be ready in an hour or so. Why don't you come back out to the farm?"

Jay-Bob did not answer right away. Betty's headache began to creep back.

"Who all is out there right now?" the deputy finally asked. "Every time I come your way, you seem to have all kinds of people around, including strangers."

"Nobody is here now," Betty said, trying to keep her voice light, upbeat. She wanted him to return to the farm with his guard down. "And I've got a little something extra-special planned for you that's got nothing to do with the food you're going to eat when we're finished."

Those words seemed to excite the deputy. Betty knew it was what he had been longing to hear for quite some time.

"I got a little paperwork to do here at the office, but then I will be right out," he said. "I'm really looking forward to seeing you alone, and I haven't had me a good dinner in a long time."

Betty clicked off the cell as Katie came back into the farmhouse, carrying a baseball bat that they'd found in the garage. It was a model named for Al Kaline, the Detroit Tigers Hall of Fame right fielder.

"We're all set," the daughter said. "Once you feed him and knock him out with this Kaline club, we'll put him through the chipper, mix him with a load of manure, and spread him out onto the fields."

"What about the deputy's cruiser?" Betty asked. She was afraid she was missing something, and her mind raced to cover all angles. "Getting rid of that asshole is one thing, but his vehicle is going to be pretty hard to hide."

"Don't worry. Travis has got it all figured out," Katie said. "He's got a chop shop in Cass City all ready to take it. Owner's had some run-ins with the cops, and he'd love to take apart a cruiser. By the end of the day, nobody will be able to find a trace of the deputy or his damn car."

Katie asked Betty how she knew Ratchett would not tip off his fellow deputies or the sheriff before he came out to the farm.

"No worry there." Betty shook her head. "He's kept our relationship a secret for more than a year. He'd be in deep trouble if word got out that he's been sneaking out here to see me on the side. Plus, he's just too lovesick," Betty said, brimming with confidence. "Jay-Bob will do just about anything I tell him. I got him wrapped around my finger."

The women laughed and high-fived. First Carl, then Tom, and now the deputy. Soon, they would be home free, and rolling in dough.

Chapter 34

Nick walked through the front door of the only German restaurant in the small village of Caro. It was between the lunch and dinner hours, so only a few customers sat at tables, sipping coffee and talking quietly. The reporter did not know what he would learn from meeting with Carl's daughters. But he thought it was worth the time and effort to find out what they knew about their dad's life—especially since Betty and her daughter had come into the picture. Besides, he liked the feistiness Carlina had displayed at the funeral.

Within a few minutes Carlina appeared. She looked like a German maiden in the full blue-and-white dress that flowed around her. It had a low-cut top, which she flowed out of. Her hair was parted down the middle and braided into pinwheels at the sides of her head. Nick thought she looked like a blond Princess Leia.

"Thanks for agreeing to meet with me," he said.

Carlina suggested they move to the lounge side of the restaurant, which was empty. She led him to a black table with heavy wooden chairs. The room was large, with red carpeting, and the windows were shuttered. The only lighting came from the bar area, though it was deserted at this hour.

"We can talk here," Carlina said. "My mom said she did not feel comfortable meeting with you. She's old school—talking about her life with Carl would not be easy. My sisters do what I tell them to do, and they're working now, getting ready for the dinner crowd."

Nick pulled out his notebook and recorder, but Carlina held up her hand. She asked that their discussion go unrecorded.

"Look, I'm happy to try and help you, but we are private, simple people," she said. "We don't want to be dragged into a big public spectacle. I don't know how much I can really help anyway."

The reporter put his recorder away and closed his notebook, saying he understood. The scene at the funeral—in front of Carl's friends and family and the media—was more than they had wanted, he was sure. He told Carlina that he was merely looking for background information on Carl's life. "New evidence indicates that your dad's passing may not have been accidental," he said.

Carlina's eyes widened, and she leaned back in her chair. After a moment she said, "I guess I shouldn't be surprised. It's what we feared all along."

The reporter tried to comfort her.

"We're just trying to make sense of what happened to your dad," he said. "When I saw you at his funeral and heard the harsh words you exchanged with Betty, well, I thought you might have something to add to the big picture."

"Betty has been his wife in name only," Carlina said, her eyes narrowing, jaw tightening. "My mom was Carl's true love and companion for all these years. When Carl brought Betty into the picture, it broke her heart. She had hoped that one day, when all his kids were grown, she could take her rightful place at his side."

Nick admitted that information about Betty and Katie was really what he'd hoped to gain from their discussion. He asked Carlina what she knew about them and how they'd come into her dad's life.

"It was a shock to us when he announced that the two of them were coming here to live with him," she said. "And from Chicago, of all places. That's what we couldn't figure out. Why would they want to make a life here, and really, how would they fit in way out here in the Thumb?"

"I know, I know," Nick said. "I grew up on a farm about twenty miles from here, so I understand the total culture shock. But then again, we do see instances where people become so disheartened by the crime, the crowds, and the pollution that they decide to give it all up and seek the peace and solitude of country life. I know folks who have come from Detroit or Cleveland or even Chicago and never looked back."

Carlina sat across from Nick, slowly shaking her head. Then she unloaded.

"But that's not what happened in this case," she said. "They never fit in and never really tried to—that's what Carl said right from the beginning. He told Mom he regretted bringing them here, but he kept saying he wanted to give them more time to adjust. I think they were only here for his money and land."

Nick hoped she had proof or could point him in a direction where he could find it. "What led you to believe that was the case?"

"Carl was not an easy man to be around," she said. "He was cranky and set in his ways. Who would put up with that if they didn't have to? Most of the time we were glad he only visited us occasionally.

"But even more than that, they didn't like the people here. Katie complained about the school and her classmates. Carl said she called them hicks and hayseeds. Betty never joined any of the local civic organizations either—just the book club in Pigeon, from what I heard. It wasn't working out, and Carl knew that, but he didn't know how to get out of it. I heard him tell Mom that many times."

Carlina stood up suddenly and apologized for not offering Nick coffee—or a glass of water or a cold pop. While she fetched beverages from the bar, Nick jotted down a few quick notes. When she returned, he closed his notebook, telling her that he was only making notes for background information that he would follow up on later.

The coffee was fresh, the aroma stimulating. Nick sipped slowly from his mug. Carlina took a man-sized gulp of her ice water and set the blue-tinted glass down in front of her.

Nick figured she was ready for more questions. He asked Carlina what she knew about Betty and Katie and whether she or her sisters had tried to find out about their pasts in Chicago.

"We're not investigators or detectives or reporters," she said. "So we really don't know too much. But I did do some nosing around on the internet when we became suspicious of their motives with Carl."

Nick asked what she'd learned, hoping there was something he could chase down with his colleagues at *The Blade*.

"Two things, really," she said. "One, both of Betty's husbands— one named Lippman and the other, Tate—they both had accidental deaths. Lippman was electrocuted, and Tate fell down his basement stairs and hit his head on the cement floor. Now, how often does one woman have two—well, three—husbands who meet untimely deaths? I've never heard of that happening."

"Interesting," Nick said, trying to act casual about the new information. He'd known about Lippman, of course, but not Tate. Nick remembered what Dave had told him about the so-called accidents that befell the husbands of Betty's friends from the Des Moines conference. Lots of guys had had accidents when Betty and her friends were in the vicinity, he thought.

Carlina leaned in toward Nick like she was eager to tell him the rest of what she knew, or thought she did. "Katie is not Betty's daughter," she said. "Now, I don't have rock-solid proof, but I do know there was no mention of her in either the Tate or Lippman obituaries. I even called the funeral home that handled the Lippman burial and asked about Katie. The funeral director said he'd never met her or heard her mentioned. That tells me she came into the picture after the first two husbands and before Betty met Carl."

Nick believed Carlina; her observations about Katie aligned with what Dave had learned from Nettie. Katie had become the wild card in the story, and the reporter thought figuring out her connection would be one of the keys to unlocking the vault of secrecy surrounding Betty Huffmann. He looked up at Carlina. "I'd say that's pretty good detective work. Very interesting."

"Please don't quote me," she said. "I only agreed to speak up because I think there's something rotten going on here, and we would like to see the truth come out. You can use the information I gave you, but please don't attach our names to it."

Nick said he would honor her request.

"But keep reading *The Blade*," he told Carlina. "I think we're going to have plenty more to write about what happened to Carl Huffmann."

Chapter 35

Deputy Jay-Bob Ratchett drummed his fingers on the side of the printer as he hovered over it in the sheriff's department squad room. He was waiting for the machine to spit out crucial information from its interstate network.

Right on cue, Prosecutor Billington walked into the squad room, shocking the deputies working at their desks. It was foreign territory to him because of his ongoing political rift with the Huron County sheriff. The two never ventured onto each other's turf.

The prosecutor clearly was not comfortable, but Deputy Ratchett had summoned him to the sheriff's den. The reason: important new information regarding the Huffmann drowning death.

"Jay-Bob, what you got?" Billington asked, looking over his shoulder in each direction to see who was watching him talk with the deputy. "It better be good. Can't remember the last time I was over here, so I hope it's worth it."

The deputy ripped off the perforated paper that rolled from the printer. He looked over it carefully, then handed it to the prosecutor.

"I think you'll be very interested in this," Jay-Bob said. "It casts a whole new light on the Huffmann case."

As the prosecutor reviewed the information, Jay-Bob gave him the background. He said he had been out at the Huffmann homestead nosing around for more evidence, as the prosecutor had requested, when he'd discovered an unfamiliar and suspicious vehicle parked in the garage. A check of the pickup truck's VIN had revealed that the vehicle was leased to a real estate broker in Chicago.

"That's where Betty and her daughter came from. Coincidence?"

Jay-Bob asked. He stepped closer to the printer and faced the prosecutor to emphasize the importance of this revelation. "I've also seen strangers at the Huffmann place. Very suspicious. I'm digging deeper and harder, but I thought you should know that there's something fishy going on at the farm."

"Damn it, Jay-Bob! Don't tell me we got the wrong guy locked up for Carl's death," Billington said. Perspiration broke out across his forehead. His face reddened. He pulled at his collar as though it had suddenly gotten tighter.

The high pitch of his voice alarmed the other deputies, who were now watching the pair at the printer. Some whispered to each other. One loyal deputy declared that he was calling the sheriff right away.

"Too early to tell exactly what's going on, but something here just ain't right," Jay-Bob said. "I'm going back out to the Huffmann farm to talk with Betty again, but I wanted to bring you into the loop before I did."

Billington shoved his hands in his pockets, hunched up his shoulders, and left the squad room, muttering to himself. He did not look well.

The deputy tucked the printout into a file on his desk. He grabbed his gear and headed out the door. Then he stepped back inside. "Robbins," he said, addressing the desk sergeant. "I'll be out at the Huffmann farm—be back in two hours."

Chapter 36

Nick pulled out onto M-24 just as his cell phone demanded his attention. He did not recognize the number but decided to answer it anyway. "Yeah, Steele here."

"Nick, hey, it's Woody from Des Moines. The seed corn guy."

Nick remembered talking with Woodrow Tipton, from the Association of American Corn Growers, about Carl Huffmann. What he couldn't figure out was why Woody would be calling him now.

"Good to hear from you, Woody. What's up?"

Woody explained that a notice had been sent out about a year ago warning of an internet company that had been involved in some questionable practices involving farmers. He said he had missed the notice when it was first circulated, but it had caught his attention after Nick's phone call inquiring about the Huffmanns.

"It didn't click with me until later," he said. "I went back and looked up the notice and thought I should call you." Woody cleared his throat. "We know it's an internet company that does research on farmers all across the country and then sells that information for a hefty price."

"What kind of farmer information?" Nick asked. "Are you talking about crop rotation? Or pesticides, herbicides—that kind of stuff?"

"Well, yeah, there's some of that, but it's really more personal information about farmers," he said. "How big their farms are, how much machinery they have, how much livestock on hand—that kind of thing."

That sounded to Nick like information about farm wealth, and he couldn't understand why someone would want to know about financial assets unless the farmer was applying for financing. He wondered what else was available for sale.

"And there's one more thing, Nick," Woody said. "In a sense they're kind of like farmers in that they harvest data. They gather all kinds of personal information too. Married, single, divorced, widowed. The individual's likes and dislikes. They reveal whether you like catsup on your scrambled eggs or jam on your toast. What's your favorite music, drink, or hobby. It's kind of like a personal profile, like what they do on the dating websites."

"Woody, what's the name of the website?"

"It's called Widow Watch."

"Oh shit!" Nick said. "So that's how Betty and her girlfriends found and hooked those farmers at your annual conference." He thought it ingenious—someone looking for a life partner could buy the information, alter their lifestyle and thinking, even their looks, and then suddenly become the match made in heaven. Soul Mates, Inc. might have been a better name for the company, Nick thought.

"Maybe, Nick. That could be it," Woody said. "I felt so bad when I reread that notice from the president. It was an alarm, and I didn't pay attention to it when it first came out. Made me sick to my stomach. Had to call."

"You did your best, Woody—don't beat yourself up. And thanks for the call."

Nick clicked off the call and pulled up the C-Man's number. He had to update his boss. The story was turning again.

Chapter 37

Jay-Bob turned his cruiser onto the Huffmanns' private drive. He crawled along the gravel road, his tires crunching the stones that were not frozen together. But he scanned the farm's horizon, looking for anything unusual, anything that seemed out of place.

Betty's erratic behavior and the presence of a stranger with a gun and drugs had made him suspicious, and Katie was the unknown factor that he had never been able to figure out. The deputy hoped his instincts were wrong. He wanted the old Betty back, the Betty he had been carrying on a wild love affair with for more than a year. He hoped that was the Betty he had just talked to on the phone.

Almost reflexively Jay-Bob parked his cruiser so that it was pointed back down the driveway. It occurred to him that he should be prepared for anything and that a fast getaway might be in the cards.

But when Betty came out of the back entrance of the farmhouse to greet him, the deputy was relieved to see her smile. She looked great too, he thought, in her short red skirt and tight gold sweater.

Just as he reached for the door handle of the cruiser, his cell phone rang. He answered it without taking his eyes off Betty. "Deputy Ratchett."

"Deputy, this is Nick Steele," the reporter said. The sound of the reporter's voice threw Jay-Bob off. He was the last person the deputy wanted to hear from. Jay-Bob almost clicked the phone off to end the conversation before it began, but decided to let Nick continue, at least for a minute or two.

"I wanted to give you a quick heads-up about some new information I learned today," Nick said. "I called the desk sergeant, and she said you were out doing some investigative work on a pending case."

"Don't really have time," he said. "I'm on department business right now. A local VIP is waiting for me as we speak."

"If you're out at the Huffmann farm, I bet I know what the P stands for."

"What kind of a crack is that?"

"I'm calling to alert you, Jay-Bob," Nick said. "The people we are dealing with in the Huffmann case are not who they seem to be. Everywhere they go, they leave bodies in their wake. I will fill you in on everything I know, but if you are out at the Huffmann place, you could be putting yourself in harm's way."

"I got it, Nick. Thanks. I know what I'm doing."

The deputy clicked off his cell and laid it on the front seat of the cruiser. He climbed out and took off his gun belt, tossing it in his empty seat next to the cell. Then he hurried into Betty's open arms.

"Hiya, Sweet Cheeks. I'm so glad you called. Missed the old Betty."

"Thanks for overlooking my rough patch, Ace," Betty said, snuggling into his shoulder under his chin. "Come on in. Dinner is all ready."

"I thought you had a little surprise for me aside from dinner," the deputy said, his voice filled with hurt and rejection. "You're not going to make me wait again, are you?"

"Ace, you know catfish is no good when it's gone cold," Betty said. "Come in and eat, and then I'll get all heated up for you next."

Jay-Bob smiled, comfortable to be with her again. He felt foolish for being so suspicious of her, though he could not shut off his cop instincts completely. Just to be certain, the deputy slowly surveyed the grounds again, scanning across to the garage and the other outbuildings near the farmhouse. It was as quiet as a morgue on a Wednesday afternoon.

The warm aroma of freshly cooked catfish and johnnycake swept across Jay-Bob as the two settled into the dining area of the kitchen. The table was ready and waiting, with one place setting—all for him. Suddenly he was completely at ease.

Jay-Bob unfolded the cloth napkin at the side of his plate while Betty brought covered container after covered container to the table before him. It was a feast fit for a king. "This is very sweet of you. All my favorites, cooked just as I like 'em." The deputy grabbed Betty's hand and kissed it gently. She patted him on the head.

Jay-Bob moaned with pleasure as he tore into the catfish. He barely noticed when after a few minutes Betty slowly drifted into the kitchen, and he did not look up when she came back into the dining area, carrying the Kaline Classic behind her back. Batter up!

But their final moment together was interrupted by the sound of a vehicle coming up the driveway. Betty stood the baseball bat on its end in a corner. Jay-Bob rose quickly, forcing his napkin to the floor.

"I thought you said we would be all alone today," he said, pushing back the window blind to examine the drive. He didn't recognize the car, an older Chevy Malibu.

"I'm not expecting anybody," Betty said. She peered out the lower part of the window just as a young man climbed out of the vehicle and walked up to the farmhouse, looking around the grounds as if it was his first viewing. He knocked on the back door that was nearest the kitchen. Jay-Bob and Betty jumped.

"I don't know who it is, honestly," Betty said, almost whispering to Jay-Bob. "Should I answer it?"

Jay-Bob nodded and stood back away from the doorway in the shadows of the pantry area. She opened the door.

"Hi, is Trevor around? My name is Gordon, and I'm from *The Bay City Blade*," the young man said. He smiled at Betty, his hands in his pockets.

"Trevor? Nobody with that name here," she said. Betty started to close the door to send the young man on his way so she could look for her bat. But the reporter continued.

"This is the address he gave me," Gordon said. "I met him out ice fishing—we partied a little together. He told me about his gun and knife collections, so I thought I'd look him up and see what he's got."

"Oh, you must mean Travis. I think he is a collector," Betty said, flustered by the appearance of the reporter at her door. She glanced back at his car, parked directly behind Jay-Bob's vehicle in the driveway. "But he's not here right now. Leave your card, and I'll give it to him."

The young man nodded. "I see you're tending to some police business," he said, motioning toward the cruiser. "I can connect with him later."

The young reporter thanked Betty for her time and turned to walk back to his vehicle just as Travis appeared from behind the barn. He was carrying a shotgun in one hand, the barrel pointed up in the air. He waved at Gordon.

"Oh my god," Betty said, clutching Jay-Bob's arm.

"Hey, good seeing you again, Gordon," Travis said. "You're looking a lot better now than you did the last time I saw you."

"What the hell is going on here?" the deputy said. He edged around Betty to get a better look. "You said we'd be alone. Looks like a convention is taking place out there."

The deputy moved to the door and recognized Travis as the young stranger he'd seen with Katie at the farm earlier. Now he was armed and talking to the kid who'd come to the door, some kind of reporter.

Jay-Bob reached for his own weapon, suddenly realizing it was in the cruiser with his cell. "Damn, I'm naked in here," he said. "Betty, any weapons in the house? Carl was a hunter, wasn't he?"

"No, I got rid of them all," she said. "I don't even know how to use one."

The deputy decided he had to go outside and take control of the situation before it got out of hand. The sight of Gordon talking to the armed stranger scared the hell out of him. He stepped out of the house and into the driveway.

"Hey there, guys. What's going on?" he said.

"Nothing, deputy. Just showing this reporter one of the guns in my collection," Travis said, smiling at Gordon, who was now standing next to him. The young reporter beamed at the collector he'd met on the ice.

"Is that weapon loaded?" Jay-Bob asked. "I'm afraid I'm going to have to ask you to put it down on the ground."

"Why yes, it is loaded," Travis said. He grabbed the reporter by the arm and pulled him in front of his chest, wrapping his free arm around Gordon's neck. He now had a hostage. "Deputy, I see you're in no position to ask me to do anything. Now, why don't you raise your hands in the air. The three of us are going to take a little walk over to the other side of the barn."

Jay-Bob raised his hands but did not move from his position. He had no intention of going anywhere near the barn. But now he had to worry about the safety of the young reporter.

"You're heading down the wrong path," Jay-Bob said. "You're holding a loaded weapon on a man. If you stop right now, you can still get out of this with no harm done. Let him go and put down the weapon. Now."

Betty moved out into the driveway. Jay-Bob saw she was not

pleased with what was happening, and she let the man with the gun know it. "Travis, what the hell do you think you are doing? Enough! This has gone too far."

"Betty, if you don't have the guts, then get your ass back in the house," Travis said, shouting now. Gordon squirmed in his head-lock. "Katie and I can handle this. Plenty of room in that chipper for two—even if we have to run 'em through twice."

Travis backed up toward the barn, pulling Gordon along with him. He ordered Jay-Bob to follow, but the deputy refused again.

"Okay, asshole, move this way *now*, or the reporter gets a face full of hot lead, and then I take you out before you can get to your vehicle."

Jay-Bob hoped a bluff would work—it had to. Even if he got to his gun belt, it only had one round of ammo. "If I don't return or call into the department, an army of cops will come out here looking for me. There's no good way out for you unless you surrender."

"You think I'm stupid," Travis said. "You didn't come out here on police work, you came to play patty-cake with Sweet Cheeks over there. Nobody knows you're here, and nobody's coming."

Standoff. Jay-Bob was not moving toward the barn, and Travis was not about to surrender to an unarmed cop. He pulled the reporter even closer. Gordon gasped for air. Betty feared the worst— bloodshed.

Just as Travis was about to say he would count to three before blowing away Gordon, four sheriff's deputy patrol cars, lights flashing, rolled down the Huffmann driveway. Minutes later a Michigan State Police helicopter came across the tree line from the opposite direction.

"Let's not do anything stupid," Jay-Bob said. "Release the kid, put down the weapon, and raise your hands."

With patrol cars forming an arc around him and his hostage,

and the chopper now hovering overhead, Travis surrendered. He was ordered to get down on the ground as deputies moved in to make the arrest.

The last vehicle pulling into the driveway was the gold Firebird belonging to Nick Steele. It was his urgent call to Prosecutor Billington that had sent the four deputies and the chopper to the Huffmann homestead.

The deputies checked out Gordon, who seemed shocked by what he had walked into. They gave him a bottled water and waited for him to calm down. Nick was flabbergasted to see the intern at the Huffmann farm. He also couldn't understand how the kid had wandered back into his story—and become a key figure in it.

"Holy shit, Gordon, what the hell are you doing out here?" he asked.

The intern took another swig of water, draining the bottle. He looked up at Nick. "I took your advice," he said. "You thought the gun and knife collector might make a good story, so I was chasing it down. I got the guy's name mixed up, but he's the one I told you about."

Nick immediately thought about Morton Reynolds and Gordon's dad. He wondered if the intern getting held hostage by a killer was similar to leaving him alone out on assignment. On the other hand, he figured he could probably use some more time off on suspension. And at least the kid would have one hell of a story to tell.

"We've got to get you out of here as soon as the deputies are done with you," Nick said. "Are you going to be okay to drive home?"

"I'm fine now, but I was scared shitless a little while ago," Gordon said, which Nick thought was fair, given what had just happened in the course of about twenty minutes. "You know, I really like being a reporter."

Nick smiled. "Me too," he said, and they watched deputies hand-cuff Travis, Katie, and Betty and lead them away.

Another patrol car rolled down the driveway. It was the sher-iff. He jumped out of the vehicle and drew his weapon. But he straightened his necktie before asking two questions: "Everything under control here?" and "Where are the TV cameras, behind the barn?"

Jay-Bob replied, telling his boss he could put away the pistol. "Everything is good. It will all be in my report. And sorry, but there are no TV cameras."

The sheriff looked crestfallen about the cameras. He told Jay-Bob to carry on and jumped back into his cruiser and sped away.

Jay-Bob approached the group, thanking Nick for calling the prosecutor. "But I really wish you'd called my boss first. Boy, is he going to be pissed when he finds out Billington made the call to the desk sergeant to send out deputies."

The two laughed. A crisis had been averted, and both men said they were happy that no one was hurt in the confrontation. They exchanged information, now forming an alliance.

Nick said he wanted to let the deputy know that the owner of the internet company selling information about farmers was a man named Tony Shultz, of Chicago.

"You don't say," Jay-Bob said. "Just so happens that there's a red Chevy pickup here that's leased to Tony Shultz of Chicago. Imagine that."

Chapter 38

On Friday morning, Drayton Clapper called the Huron County prosecutor and gave him a rundown on the stories that would be running in that day's paper. The newsroom chief was doing this as a courtesy to the prosecutor, but he also hoped the revelations would prompt fresh comment from the Huron lawman.

Clapper said one story would expose a national internet-based conspiracy that had hit home in Huron County with the death of Carl Huffmann. The other piece would summarize Nick's interview with Tom Huffmann, telling the full story of what had happened out on Wild Fowl Bay. Another article, written by a young local freelance writer, would tell of the allure of ice fishing and why it was so popular and potentially dangerous.

"You know, I've had a rotten feeling about this case since it came to my desk," Preston Billington said. A long pause settled between the men. "What have you got?" His voice was filled with anticipation, but he was worried about how the news reports would reflect on him. "I don't want to look like a fool, and I'm hanging on by my fingertips politically here."

"Well, I can't let you read the story or alter it before publication," Clapper said. "But I could read you what we are publishing this morning, and you can decide what you want to do from there."

"Sounds like a deal," Boney Fingers said, scratching his head and letting thousands of particles of dandruff loose in his office. "I will not interrupt."

Clapper cleared his throat and read the conspiracy story to Billington. When the C-Man finished, Boney Fingers had a one-word response: "Damn!"

The prosecutor asked Clapper to transfer him to Nick Steele's phone in the newsroom. "I'm going to tell your guy that I'm releasing Tom Huffmann. He should be out in time to read your paper when it hits the streets."

The C-Man completed the transfer.

When *The Blade* published later that morning, the Huffmann saga took up three quarters of the front page.

Accused killer released; Blade probe reveals Huron's Huffmann died in national conspiracy to steal farms

By Nick Steele and Dave Balz

The Huron County prosecutor dropped charges against Thomas Huffmann and released him from jail today after a probe by The Bay City Blade revealed that his father died in a conspiracy orchestrated by the leader of a Chicago-based company.

The goal of the company, investigators said, was to help their customers seize control of family farms and then sell off the land and their assets.

Preston Billington, Huron County prosecutor, said justice was served with the release of Tom Huffmann. The prosecutor said his office had been in contact with the FBI's Cyber Division and that those who had conspired in the death of Carl Huffmann had been arrested and faced charges of homicide and conspiracy.

"The FBI is involved because this is a national, and perhaps an international, conspiracy," Billington said. "Some really bad actors came into our community with the goal of killing one of our own and stealing his family farm."

Tony "the Tiger" Shultz is listed as the owner of the internet-based Widow Watch. The company compiles research on rich farmers – male and female – across the United States and sells the information for thousands of dollars.

Huron County's Carl Huffmann, and others, including a farmer from Ohio and another from Wisconsin, died recently from what appeared to be accidents after they met women at a Des Moines, Iowa, seed corn conference. The women had purchased information from Widow Watch and hired consultants through the company.

Huffmann died while he and his son, Tom, were on an ice-fishing expedition out on Wild Fowl Bay. The two men broke through the ice on their 4-wheelers. The younger Huffmann made it to shore and was aided by the Thompson family of Sand Point.

Rescuers tried to save the elder Huffmann, but he could not be revived after his body was discovered the following morning, tangled in weeds in about eight feet of water.

Investigators say they believe Huffmann was able to pull himself out of the water but was struck on the head with a crescent wrench by Travis Benson, a consultant for Widow Watch, who had tracked the Huffmanns out onto the ice. Carl Huffmann is believed to have been knocked unconscious by the blow to his head, and later drowned.

Benson and his brother were hired by Betty Huffmann to help her reorganize the farm she took over after Carl's death.

Travis Benson, Katie MacDonald, and Betty Huffmann were arrested after a brief standoff with deputies and the state police at the Huffmann homestead. Benson had taken Blade reporter Gordon Smith hostage, holding a shotgun to his head. Smith was not harmed during the standoff, but his father, Robert J. Smith, a local bank president, fell into a catatonic state when he learned of his son's involvement in the case. The elder Smith has remained unresponsive but sometimes blinks when his son utters the word "Daddy."

MacDonald was believed to be Betty Huffmann's daughter from a previous relationship, but investigators have not discovered any familial relationship between the two. MacDonald is reportedly the spouse of Benson, who met her when she worked as a nude dancer in a Chicago gentleman's club.

Investigators are now looking into the deaths of Walter Dupinski of Prairie Farm, Wisconsin, and Edgar Truscott of Amanda, Ohio. They met, and later married, friends of Betty Huffmann at the same Des

Moines conference where Carl Huffmann met Betty.

Both men died in farm accidents. Dupinski was electrocuted in his workshop, and Truscott fell into a running combine. Their wives had purchased information from Widow Watch and hired farm reorganization consultants through the agency.

Since the deaths of Dupinski and Truscott, their farms and equipment have been sold at auction. Both wives and their consultants have disappeared.

Billington also told The Blade that Huron County Sheriff's Deputy J.R. Ratchett played a crucial role in developing the case against Benson, MacDonald, and Betty Huffmann.

"If the sheriff is smart, and there has never been any indication that he is, Deputy Ratchett will be up for a commendation and perhaps a promotion," he said. "We're downright proud of the work Booger did on this case."

Ratchett was humbled by the prosecutor's comments, insisting that he was just doing his job. "Not sure about the idea of a promotion," he told reporters, "but I really would like a second live bullet to store in my holster – just in case I get into another tough scrape."

Tom Huffmann said he was delighted to be out of jail. He said he had confidence the culprits in his father's death would be prosecuted and sent to prison. For now Tom looks forward to picking up the pieces with his family.

"During Dad's funeral, I learned that I have stepsisters," he said. "We have a lot of healing to do. I want to move forward with them and my brothers in a positive, constructive way."

Chapter 39

Nick and Dave drove to the Thumb together on the Sunday morning after the story broke in Friday's newspaper. They each had big plans for the day.

Their first stop was the Shear Crazy Salon in Pigeon. Dave jumped out of the Firebird and headed for the front door, where Tammy, the stylist who had actually given the reporter a little style, greeted him. They had made plans to pick up Nettie in Tammy's van and take her out to brunch. Dave liked both women very much and wanted to give them a special treat for being so kind to him. He had other plans for Tammy later that afternoon, but the boundaries of good taste and decency prevent them from being revealed.

Nick drove on to the Thompson cottage on Sand Point, where Nice Nurse Nora had invited him to join her and her family for Sunday chicken dinner. They would also conclude the interview Nick had started with her before the Ice Man banged on her door.

When Nick arrived at the cottage, the Thompsons gave the reporter a friendly welcome, even warmer than the welcome he'd received when he first visited the cottage. The place looked exactly the same. Even the Christmas tree lights twinkled under a gray, overcast sky. Light snow gave the setting a holiday feel.

Nora told Nick she had exciting news to share. She said Tom had told her that he had been talking with his stepsisters, Carlina, Carla, and Carlotta, about their restaurant in Caro and the family farm.

"Tom said he was going to continue partnering with them on their German restaurant," Nora said with evident delight. "But here's the best part—turns out that Carlina has a teenage son and Carla has a daughter nearly the same age. They're going to work for Tom on the farm this summer. Isn't that great?"

"Yes, it is—a pretty interesting and wild turn of events," Nick said.

He was tickled at how it had turned out, and especially impressed with the way Tom was trying to bring his family together. All of the Huffmanns' skeletons had been pulled out of the closets. The web of secrets and behind-the-scenes scheming had been exposed. Perhaps, the reporter thought, Tom was trying to fulfill the role of father figure and family patriarch that had escaped his dad.

They settled into the cottage's living room overlooking Wild Fowl Bay, but Nick did not speak for several minutes, allowing himself time to absorb the tranquilizing view of the lake. The warm aroma of roasting chicken filled the air. A hot coal popped in the fireplace, sending crackling sparks up the chimney. Out in the distance, ice anglers moved about, looking for the next lucky hole.

The two moved ahead with their interview, which was initially what had brought them together. Both knew that before long Tom Huffmann would be banging on the cottage door again. But this time he would not be joining them, covered in snow and ice, from the lakeside of the cottage.